A LIFE

Books by Wright Morris

Novels
A LIFE
WAR GAMES
FIRE SERMON
IN ORBIT
ONE DAY
CAUSE FOR WONDER
WHAT A WAY TO GO
CEREMONY IN LONE TREE
LOVE AMONG THE CANNIBALS
THE FIELD OF VISION
THE HUGE SEASON
THE DEEP SLEEP
THE WORKS OF LOVE
MAN AND BOY
THE WORLD IN THE ATTIC
THE MAN WHO WAS THERE
MY UNCLE DUDLEY

Photo-Text
LOVE AFFAIR: A VENETIAN JOURNAL
GOD'S COUNTRY AND MY PEOPLE
THE HOME PLACE
THE INHABITANTS

Essays
A BILL OF RITES, A BILL OF WRONGS, A BILL OF GOODS
THE TERRITORY AHEAD

Anthology
WRIGHT MORRIS: A READER

A LIFE

by
WRIGHT MORRIS

HARPER & ROW, PUBLISHERS

NEW YORK   EVANSTON   SAN FRANCISCO

LONDON

Designed by Luba Litwak

Library of Congress Cataloging in Publication Data

Morris, Wright, 1910-

A life.
I. Title.
PZ3.M8346Li   813'.5'2   73-4155
ISBN 0-06-013079-2

For Winona Osborn 1888–1973

ONE

From the highway to the east, where his car is parked to the left of a mailbox propped in a milk can, we can see him standing in the knee-high grass at the edge of a field of grain stubble. He stoops, one hand at the small of his back, in the manner of old men who find it painful. A grove of cottonwood trees, blighted or drought-killed, rises about him like masts with half-furled sails. The old man was born in this country, and it might be misleading to say that he had left it. If asked if he could use a pair of shoes, he would reply, I have a pair of shoes. We see them on his feet. They are high-top shoes, with box toes, the metal hooks and eyes hard on the laces. He wears out more laces than anything else. Neither shoes nor laces are what they used to be, and neither are his feet. The car we see back on the highway is a Maxwell coupe, acquired in exchange for a Dodge touring in 1928. He could use a better car, and will think about buying one when this one wears out. The grass he stands in is green compared to the yellow grain stubble, and might be classed as weeds by the men who farm the land. It's not a grass they mow, or a grain they harvest, so it must be weeds. This man is old enough to know better and remember when it was grass from horizon to horizon. His father had taken grass, as he did most things, religiously. Before the land had been plowed, or some would say broken, he had distinguished a dozen or more varieties of land cover, the nameless grasses that kept the soil from washing and blowing away. One thing he showed his son was how the shorter the grass, the longer the roots. Reluctant to heed or learn anything from his father, the boy had learned that. He knew that the tall bluestem slashed his legs like sabers, and made cuts between his toes that itched like crazy. He liked the sour grass from the way it tasted and the blue grama from the way it sounded, along with buffalo grass, big and little bluestem, and the tall, sweet-stemmed switch grass, as good as its name. Wheat, too, was grass, along with barley, oats, and rye, and on the same authority the

2

tall corn was grass, but the pleasure of the grassland was diminished if everything growing on it proved to be grass, except for the trees. It pained the old man, as a boy, to watch the grazing cattle jerk their heads upward to tear loose a patch of cord grass, a stem of which he holds, the head wagging, between his teeth. In his mind, thanks to his father, the word of God is tangled with the names of grasses, and the mention of one evokes the other. Being as old as he is, he thinks of that and the paleness of the grass on the grave of his sister, green as winter wheat. Dead now three weeks, the last of the family, excepting himself. "How is my darling old scoffer?" she would ask him. For weeks now nobody has asked him. It occurs to him that from now on nobody ever will.

His name is Warner, but people refer to him as "the old man." "You mean the old man with the kid?" they would say, although the boy was only his kin by marriage. It occurs to him that from now on he would not hear that, either. The boy had taken off with a pair of hippies picked up on the road. Warner had been born and raised in this country, but as soon as he was raised he had left it. He had not liked it much then; he did not like it now. Even as a boy he had learned to stand with his back to the wind.

Just ten days ago he had left California to come back here and settle the affairs of his sister, who had recently died. Now they were settled, his sister was buried, and what she couldn't take with her had gone up in smoke. As for the boy, Warner would check to see if there were people locally on the mother's side of his family—Holtorfer by name, once said to be from Archer. Warner would tell them what had happened, and where, if they wanted him, they might find him. Would the boy ever believe that Warner would be relieved to find them all dead?

On the south side of Archer, where he stopped to buy gas, he mentioned the name Holtorfer to the station attendant. He learned that one Holtorfer, a Miss Effie Mae, old now and a little dim-witted, lived with a Miss Amanda Plomer. To the gas man's knowledge she had always lived with her, but how would he know since she was older than he was? Surely Warner had heard of Effie Mae's brother, Ivy, the last man in the county to be killed by Indians. Warner had not heard it, but now that he had heard it he thought it highly unlikely. As a boy, he had seen more gypsies than Indians, and they scared him worse. Effie Mae, a little girl at the time, had never got over what had happened. Now that she was old, nothing else seemed to occupy her mind. For years now Amanda Plomer, a religious-type lady who had never married, looked after her. The two ladies managed better living together, since they could pool their Social Security money and keep only one house.

The elm blight had ravaged the town south of the tracks, but left the north, and poorer side of town, in the shade. After so many years in California, Warner found the elm-lined street like a tunnel, almost a strain to his eyes. The first house on the block, recently repainted a white that seemed luminous in the darkness, sat flat on the ground, the baseboards trimmed with grass out of reach of the mower. On the track side of the house the shades were drawn as if to reduce the racket of a passing freight train. A woman came to the screen to watch Warner pass, as if the sound of the Maxwell was familiar to her. The Holtorfer place, a cottage-type dwelling, was more or less concealed by two huge lilac bushes at the front. The clapboards on the visible side of the house were so free of paint they were like boards in a walk, or a weather-beaten fence. So much time had passed since the lilacs were trimmed, the upper branches formed an arch at the entrance to the porch, like trees planted at the door to a tomb. The yard grass had grown so thick and matted it provided a billowy hay-colored carpet, spongy with the growth of grass that tried and failed to reach the light. At the front of the yard blocks of the sidewalk tilted to accommodate the elm roots, but it seemed clear that the tenants walked in and out of the driveway to the door at the back. In Warner's boyhood only hobos used the door at the back, so he thought it better to use the one at the front. A thread spool (it pleased Warner to see it) had replaced the handle to the screen, the holes kicked through it at the bottom patched with pieces of shoe-box cardboard. In the cool of the shade, the draft from the house was like that from an old icebox empty of ice. Just inside the door, sprawled so flat on the couch he thought it a dress put out for airing, a woman lifted her arms toward him as the porch boards creaked.

"It's Will!" she called. "Is that you, Will?"

Before Warner could reply, from a room at the back a figure came toward him he thought to be a crippled child. The walk was that of a creature accustomed to crutches, or trained to get along without mechanical braces. She, too, her arms extended, called out to him in a voice like a parrot. Warner stopped in his tracks, an arm's length from the door, unable

6

to move forward or backward. He watched her toddle toward him, push open the screen, then grasp him about the hips like a child. Warner reached to his back to release her hands, but she held him tight. Sometimes the very old, reduced to skin and bones, give an impression of unusual strength. She held him fast, her frizzled hair tickling his face. The woman on the couch, seeing that he was not Will, had pushed herself up and come out on the porch to persuade the little one to release him. It was not easy, but the way she went about it, her voice calm, her manner assured yet gentle, suggested to Warner this sort of greeting was more commonplace than unusual.

"Effie Mae thinks you're her daddy," she said to Warner, "she thinks gentlemen callers are her daddy."

Effie Mae had stepped back to see clearly who he was: the look she gave Warner led him to wonder. Short frizzly bobbed hair stuck out from her temples, straight up from her scalp. The startled look this gave her seemed at odds with her pleasure in seeing him. She might have been Warner's age, or half again his age, suds dried on her arms as high as her elbows, the strings of the apron she wore dragged behind her like harness traces.

"You're him," she pronounced, "you're just older."

Amanda Plomer said, "She frightens people, she's so possessive. She's never got over losing Ivy."

The word "losing," otherwise so ordinary—everybody spoke of losing someone—tallied with Warner's impression, the day before, that he had lost in the last few days a part of himself, measurable as weight. It seemed unlikely, however, that Effie Mae would ever lose what she fastened her grip on.

"At least the Indians didn't get you," she said to Warner, "did they?"

"No, ma'am," Warner said, and turned to smile at Amanda.

"Effie Mae's not forgetful," Amanda said, "of anything she chooses to remember." She returned his gaze, smiling serenely. Warner was thinking if people lived long enough, would they all look alike? He had not seen his sister in more than forty years, but he could guess how much she looked like Amanda Plomer, her straw-colored hair thin to baldness at the back of her skull. In her pale blue eyes, the mild radiance of her manner, he felt she approximated Viola in saintliness. "You're Mitchell, aren't you?" she said. "Desmond's uncle?"

Warner shook his head. No, he was not Desmond's uncle, so far as he knew. He was related, by mar-

riage, to Hazel Holtorfer, who in turn had married a
Vernon Oelsligle, and on their death in a car accident a year ago, their son Kermit, a boy of ten, had
come to live with him. This boy he had brought with
him from California in the hope of finding some of
his own people. Both ladies were attentive. Warner
assumed that Amanda's silence was that she found it
so upsetting. On the ribs revealed by her dress she
moved the tips of her fingers, as if stroking a wash-
board. Had he forgotten that women of Viola's faith
found very little seriously upsetting? "He's met up
with some younger people," Warner said, "more his
own age. His next of kin should know he's off my
hands."

"Holtorfer?" repeated Amanda.

Warner nodded.

Effie Mae cried, "You tell him about Ivy? You tell
him they buried him where they killed him?"

"There's Ivy Holtorfer," Amanda said, "if he had
lived. Otherwise there's just Effie Mae. . . ." Her
eyes scanned the room as if she might have overlooked
someone.

"Of the Warners," he replied, "there's just me.
It's not natural for a boy to live in a trailer cooped
up with a man as old as I am. Along the road we

picked up these young people, and it was natural for him to fall in with them. Now he's off my hands." He rubbed the palms of his hands together.

Did Amanda Plomer find that of interest? The yellow fingers of one hand passed before her eyes as if searching for strands of loose hair, but found none.

"The boy needs raising. He needs an older woman." But once he had said it, it led him to wonder. The boy would deny it. The hippie girl was as old a woman as he would like. Young people had learned to make do with each other, to do without the old. "He's off my hands," Warner repeated. "I left him with his friends back in Chapman."

The gaze of Amanda Plomer, who stood facing the door, was fixed on a figure too large for the opening. To peer in, she stooped, pressing the bulge in the screen inward. At her side, a handbag dangling on its strap to her shoe tops, a creature with a spread-legged stance peered to the right and the left, in a birdlike manner. In her free hand she gripped a folded newspaper, which she used to fan the air.

"Mrs. Lindblatt! Miss Belle!" said Amanda. "Do come in."

"We didn't know you had company," replied the tall one. The screen open, she stepped to one side to let the smaller one precede her. Effie Mae moved to take a firm grip on Warner's arm.

"He's mine," she said. "You can't have him."

Rather than dwarf those who stood in the same room with her, Mrs. Lindblatt stood back, waiting to be encouraged to step forward. "He wouldn't be if he knew what it meant, would he?" Did this refer back to Effie Mae's statement? Mrs. Lindblatt's broad face lacked both features and expression. The lids of her eyes were swollen, as if stung by bees.

Miss Belle said, "I smell chocolate chip cookies."

"Not today," replied Amanda, "perhaps Wednesday or Friday."

As if a voice called her from the kitchen, Miss Belle started for it, her handbag swinging.

Mrs. Lindblatt said, "If she gets ahold of something, she brings it bad luck. Look what happened to Cleo. Look what happened to Honey."

Amanda turned her gaze on Effie Mae, who strengthened her grip on Warner. "What did happen?" she asked.

"They died," said Mrs. Lindblatt, "didn't anybody tell you?"

"Things slip her mind," said Amanda.

"She handled them too much," said Mrs. Lindblatt.

11

"You can't handle kittens the way you do some things. It gets their insides jumbled." She looked behind her, then around her. "Miss Belle, where you at?" Miss Belle had disappeared. Unhurried, touching objects as she passed, touching the plants that crowded the sunny window, where artificial birds were perched on sticks, Miss Amanda entered the kitchen. A moment later, with Miss Belle, she reappeared, Miss Belle clutching a sprouting potato. Was it her eyes sparkling, or the light on her glasses?

"She don't eat it," said Mrs. Lindblatt, "she hoards it. You ought to see her room. It's like a fruit cellar."

Amanda said, "Well, bless her heart. She can have it if she wants it."

Effie Mae cried, "She can't have him. He's mine!" and tightened her grip on Warner. Amanda stooped to help Miss Belle add the potato to the contents of her handbag.

"*White* bread?" Amanda asked, holding up a bread wrapper.

"For birds," replied Mrs. Lindblatt. "Some birds like it."

Warner said, "If you ladies will excuse me—" but his effort to move was checked by Effie Mae.

"Don't let her get a grip on you," said Mrs. Lindblatt. "It's bad luck." Amanda turned to Warner, lifting his arm to gently pry loose Effie Mae's gripping fingers. Effie Mae watched, as if unaware that the hand was her own. Her fingers had left their impression on Warner's wrist, white bands the blood was slow to return to. "If you ladies will excuse me—" he repeated, but Amanda gave no sign that she had heard him, and turned away to make a clear space in the center of the room. Chairs were moved back, and Warner thought for a moment she meant to recite to them, or sing. Mrs. Lindblatt and Miss Belle had played the game before, however, and stepped forward to offer their hands to Amanda. Warner's right hand was gripped by Miss Belle, and his left by Effie Mae, so that they formed a circle.

"God protect him from Indians!" cried Effie Mae.

"Not so fast, dear," replied Amanda. They stood holding hands, observing the silence, attentive to Miss Amanda's concentration. She had lowered her head, allowing it to tilt slightly to one side. In repose, Effie Mae's slack-jawed face seemed larger, the wide eyes like those in a mask, the hands dangling at her sides like clumps of roots. The tilt of Amanda's face exposed to Warner a profile like that of a dreaming child. Behind the lids the eyes were moving. Warner could not explain the tremor, like a chill, that began at his fingers and passed through his body, affecting him so powerfully that his knees trembled. He glanced upward to see, pinned to the rafters, postcards and pictures of a religious nature, the details somewhat blurred by the film on his eyes. For the second time in twenty-four hours what Warner knew to be commonplace seemed strange, and what he knew to be bizarre seemed commonplace. His hands held by these gentle elderly ladies, in a manner he knew to be childish, he felt a child's terror that if Effie Mae released his hand he would rise toward the ceiling. This would surprise no one. The giant Mrs. Lindblatt would put her hand up and pull him down. That this would surely happen led his limbs to tremble, so that Effie Mae took a firmer grip on him.

"I'm scared for him!" she cried, jarring Amanda out of her trance.

"You can let him go, dear," Amanda calmly replied. "There's nothing can happen that hasn't already happened," to which she added, "Amen."

"Amen," echoed Mrs. Lindblatt and Miss Belle. Something in what Amanda had said escaped Warner, but it seemed to reassure Effie Mae. She released Warner's hand, and watched it rise to rest, gently, on her frizzled hair. The impression that his life flowed into her was so manifest that he trembled. It would not have surprised him if he had fallen, or risen, effortlessly, toward the rafters. Effie Mae did not seize him when he turned and walked to the door. He let himself out, without glancing back, and no sound came from the house to indicate they were watching. "He's buried where they killed him!" Effie Mae pronounced, as if in answer to a question put to her. Warner's first glance back was from the turn at the corner, where the spear pointing to heaven, on the lightning rod, appeared appropriate to all that had happened.

What had it been? Two or three miles south of town, the prayer ceremony had left his mind fuzzy, like a blow on the head. He let the car straddle the center of the road, like a horse that knew its way home better than he did. Through the cranked-down window a cooling breeze dried his damp face. Just before the house had burned down, and he was still in it, like a ghost in the upstairs bedroom, he had experienced a similar sensation. The weakness in his limbs had led him to sag to a chair, facing the cracked blind and yellow light at the window. His impression had been that his eyes, his *own* eyes, hovered above him like a presence, seeing the things of this world about him for the first time. The view from the window, framed like a painting, impressed him as timeless and unchanging, and the old man seated on the armless rocker was within the scene, not outside of it. For a fleeting, breathless moment he took himself for dead. This sensation was more agreeable than unpleasant, a moment of suspended animation, recalling to his mind the silence that followed the singing of a hymn. *I'm crossing the bar*, he thought, *crossing the bar*. This seizure lasted only a moment but it left him pleasurably addled. Did he hear a voice ask him, "Old man, how are you?" or did he put such a question to himself? His opinion was he was still as good as might be expected, had been for years. The query "Who's next?" put to him like a barber, might pop into his head at the least likely moment. The crux of the matter was all in whether he replied, "He is," or, "I am." It hardly seemed to matter. To the query, "Old man, are you crazy?" he has both a smile and a ready answer. He may well be crazy, but he's certainly no crazier than anybody else.

As a small boy, twirled in a swing until he felt queasy and the world tilted, his return to normalcy had been accompanied by a sense of weightlessness, as if in twirling he had lost something. He felt that way now. It had come over him, like a mild illness, so common to his sisters before they fainted, as he stood in the prayer circle, his hands held by the women. Was it common to people made dizzy by twirling, or by prayer, to inwardly smile? For a brief moment did they feel free of this world, like children tossed in a blanket? If prayer did this for people, it was something that his sister had never mentioned. He had never once said to her, as he might now, "I know how you feel." How she felt was free, disembodied, outside herself. Warner had felt it. That he continued to feel it led him to straddle the road and drive slowly. If he zigzagged on the highway would they think him drunk? Off to the left—would that be east? he had lost confidence in his bearings—a cluster of abandoned farm buildings sat in a grove of dying cottonwoods. A weedy, winding lane, like a dried-up creek bed, led back to the road where the turnoff was marked by a mailbox propped up in a milk can. The lid of the box gaped open, and he could see that it was still stuffed with circulars. He let the car drift by, then brought it to a halt to check the side of the box facing the direction of delivery. Worn away, but guessable, if you know what you are reading, like the weathered MAIL POUCH sign on a barn roof, was the name D. Ho torfe . No *l* at all, nor much *r* at the end, but if you know what to look for you could supply it, as Warner did. He left the car and walked back to check it, just to be sure. Curiously, it was easier to read at a distance, but Holtorfer it was. Warner did not of course believe what such a coincidence suggested, but he would have liked to have shared it with Viola. "You see," she would have said, "you old scoffer!" He loved to hear her say "scoffer." Such things were coincidences, they happened all the time, and his coming along this road was one of them.

The Holtorfer place was being farmed by a neighbor who had left some of his machinery in the yard. Warner stopped beside a wagon, the floor sprinkled with wheat grains the size and color of mice turds. The sheds and barns lay to the south, the barn dilapidated, the roof sunken so that it looked like an ailing monster, bats hanging from the rafters where Warner could see them through the unhinged door. He did not like bats. The eerie whisper of their wings brushing his face had scared him silly when he was a boy and slept on an open porch. Bushes had grown at both ends of the porch and he knew bats were crossing by the movements of the leaves in the breath of their wings. The Holtorfer house depressed him, all the windows broken by hoodlums for the pleasure of hearing the glass crackle, and he walked wide around it as if it were haunted. The trees were dying, as he had seen from the road, their top branches sticking up into the sky like fingers, but the lower branches provided foliage to darken the grove and keep weeds from growing. Cows had had the run of the place for some time, the ground spongy with their crumbling droppings. Shady groves of cottonwoods had been rare on the plains in Warner's boyhood, and they would soon be rare again now that the groves were dying. The land they occupied could be plowed and seeded with wheat or corn. At the west end of the grove, where the sun got at them, there were clumps of weeds just out of reach of the plows. Warner was drawn by the light at the end of the grove, nothing more. As he approached, the view widened to include the green village of Archer, he tripped on a post in the knee-high weeds, paused a moment to curse. Back on his feet, but still tipped over, one hand at the small of his back to assist him, he saw that the post was a piece of stone about the size of a table leg. Such things were once used to determine claims, establish boundaries. This one, of moss-greened marble, had on its top the initials IH, plain as a cattle brand.

It was at this moment we first saw him from the road, where he had parked his car, his profile like that of a man relieving himself. The time he took, allowing for his age, was longer than that. It took time— his condition being somewhat light-headed—for the pieces to come together and register on him their proper effect. He had stumbled on the grave of Ivy Holtorfer, believed to be the last white man in the county to be killed by Indians, his age seventeen. The stone had no date, two sides marble smooth, two rough with a pelt of moss. Deeper in the grass he found a rusted can containing a piece of crumpled tin foil. Since the age of tin foil, that is to say, someone had come here with an offering of flowers. All of Warner's long life this youth had lain here dead to all that had happened, dead to all that would ever happen, dead to even the fact of birth and dying, since killed by Indians as he stood daydreaming, or stooped over a plow. Warner's feelings, if he had cared to admit them, were so bizarre as to be ghoulish. Ivy Holtorfer seemed as real to him as himself. Not only in his youth, that of a boy who had all of his life before him, but also in the predicament of his death. Had he looked up, or failed to look up, before the bullet or the arrow had found him? If Warner did not, one could only say that he lacked the strength. The presence of his own death was so real it awed more than it scared him. As if held by the hand, bemused by voices, inwardly smiling at the novelty of it, all the deaths of this world that had escaped him, mother and wife, five loving sisters, one so fresh in her grave little grass grew on it, he was able to grasp the irretrievable loss to Ivy Holtorfer of his own unlived life. It shamed him to think how little of life he had yet to lose.

Is he so old as that? He's eighty-two, but with Viola gone he has no proof. It astonished and pleased him that no living person could testify to his age, only the dead. If he so desired he could pick a new one. He might say he was up to ten years younger, as people often remarked. A man in Santa Cruz had made a new life for himself by declaring he recalled the sight of Lincoln, at the end of the Civil War. Any fool with eyes in his head knew he was lying. Warner recalled Buffalo Bill, on his white horse, leading the Hagenback and Wallace circus into Schuyler, the envy of kids who had never set eyes on a buffalo.

21

When Warner told that story to his nephew, Kermit, the boy had replied, "Who's Buffalo Bill?" It hadn't seemed a good question to Warner at the time, but now it did.

TWO

The name of Warner is well known in Merrick County, Nebraska, where Myron Warner settled a homestead on the bluffs south of the Platte, and the town of Chapman would have borne the Warner name, or that of Osborn, his wife's name, if she had not feared to offend the Lord with such a show of pride. Five of the Warners' surviving children, all of them girls, learned to love God and fear Him, but the son and firstborn refused to observe the Adventist sabbath or accept any day as holy. Even as a boy he hated his father, and equally loved and pitied his mother, seldom out of bed with unwanted children. On the Adventist sabbath he often stayed in his room and read the works of Colonel Ingersoll, the great agnostic. At fifteen, slight of build but active (the Warners ran small, but never stopped running), he hired himself out as a threshing hand and left his father's house never to return. That same summer, a few weeks later, he had the first of the loving, taunting letters from his sister, and in return sent her the first of the numberless postcards ridiculing everything and anything she believed, or he feared she might happen to believe. These letters, filed in shoe boxes, salvaged from the attic of the homestead, were among the items and perishable objects that went up in smoke the previous evening, traces of the smoke still visible in the morning, dimming the lights of Grand Island off to the west, and the Pony Express stop nine miles to the east. The Pony Express had ceased, of course, with the railroad, the gleaming two-way track bed of the Union Pacific. In these spare facts there is much of Warner's history. He saw railroads come, he saw horses go, he once rode in a Franklin with its air-cooled engine (this before his own home had indoor plumbing) and sixty years later he drives, when it will run, a 1927 Maxwell coupe. Now that it is no longer pulling the trailer it seems to have a lot of pep, but the body rattles. Like a kite without a tail, the motor acts skittish when going downgrade, or caught in a tailwind. He has to keep a firmer grip on the wheel than he used to, his eyes on the road.

Has he aged overnight, or is that an idle question, already being too old to begin with? Is he so old that having aged overnight means nothing, except in his head?

Viola would ask him, "How is my old darling?"

How is he? He is old.

The day before, of all the days of his life, just a few hours in time and a few miles in space, had been the most eventful. He had seen the past, lock, stock, and barrel, go up in smoke. A column of hot air, rippling like water, had risen from the blackened yard where the house had stood, lofting ashes and pieces of debris to where the cooler breeze had set them blazing. The beams of car lights, parked back in the trees, had crisscrossed at that point where the house had vanished, like footlights playing on a stage. At the center of the stage, two small figures had cast huge shadows on the barn behind them. The very sight of them had aroused Warner's fury. Everything that had happened, everything yet to happen, could be laid at the feet—at least two of them dirty—of that pair of kids. As he knew it would, and as it always had, one goddam thing always led to another, and this was the last in the series that dissolved his past into a column of air. And *that* event was now receding before he had managed to grasp it clearly, like something that caught his eye at the car window, displaced, a moment later, by something else. An event that was nearest to him in time now proved to be to its disadvantage. The wheel of his life having come full circle, the past was now coming toward him as the present mysteriously receded. What had happened last night fell away, slipped away, like the road visible in the rear-view mirror, but what had happened in the distant past flowed toward him like objects approaching on the highway.

Where was he now? With the sun on his right, he was driving south on route 183. Where that leads he'll know when he gets there. One thing he never told the boy, and would now never have to, was that he once got up at dawn, in Liberal, Kansas, and drove eighty-five miles before the sun came up where he thought it should set. That added up to one hundred and seventy miles of wrong road, all of it pretty bad. Give or take a county line, the route he was now on he had first taken in a topless buggy to pick up his bride-to-be in Oberlin, Kansas. Then with her and her dog, a little half-breed spitz that took weeks to

get used to Warner, they took sixteen days, not push-
ing the horse, to get to the homestead on the Pecos
River, just east of Roswell, New Mexico. Then it
took him almost half a day to find what little it was
he had left there. Just forty years ago he had left
more, but would it prove easier to find?

It was a comfort to Warner to be off the freeway
and back on a road where the turns were at right
angles. One reason he had put the car up on blocks
in California was that the winding roads were con-
fusing. In the space of ten miles the sun in his eyes
would be around at his back. The lack of any right
angles made it difficult for him to find his bearings.
With the angles gone, what did a man have left but
up and down? It now occurred to him that up or
down pretty well covered his available options, up to
heaven with Viola, or straight to hell with everybody
else.

The car appeared to stand still as the road swept
beneath it, spinning the wheels. Coming toward him,
from shadow into sunlight, the "memory" of lumber
for a house, brought out from Omaha on a flatcar,
dumped in the knee-high weeds along the track bed.
From there it will be floated across the spring-flooded
river, then dragged up the bluffs by a team of lame

oxen, exchanged for a wagon by people headed west-ward. What is the lumber for? To build a house on the bluffs. In his haste to complete this house for his wife, who is expecting, the builder forgets to put in the stairs between the first and second floor. A hole has to be sawed in the ceiling of the kitchen, a ladder inserted, as into a barn loft. That Warner should "remember" this is amazing, since he was the child the woman was carrying, and this was why he was born in the kitchen, and not upstairs. All of her children will be born in the kitchen, then carried up the ladder to grow up. The father is too busy running a farm, the mother is too busy bearing children, to take time out to restore the missing stairway. Besides, the children like it the way it is. Floyd Warner's first memories—as distinct from what he has heard—are of heads popping up through the hole in the floor, like a jack-in-the-box. In the kitchen he sees the ladder against a blaze of light, like a trellis, the rough steps fuzzy with the wool of their mittens and stock-ings. The draft that blows through this hole in the winter gives them all colds. Peering through it—is he a child or a boy?—he sees several women seated at a quilting frame, their heads bowed, the backs of their necks exposed. If he married Muriel Dosey—and not one of the Claytons, big soft girls who needed a man's help up and down from a buggy—it was because he had seen Muriel Dosey baptized in the Platte River, near Chapman, her slip clinging, her neck and shoulders exposed when she dipped and then popped out of the water, gasping for air. The copper glint of her skin was due (it was rumored) to the one-quarter Indian blood in her veins.

It occurs to him now, more than sixty years later, that he seldom again saw so much of her uncovered. She had been baptized. What other reason for exposing herself to men's eyes?

Warner is old, but he sees her as clearly as if he had left that riverbank this morning, and had the sand in his shoes. Others have been baptized, the men have waded to where they stand, knee deep, in the shallows, but the women, including his wife, prefer the concealment of the deeper water. The Clayton girl, Maude, covers with her hair the bust that floats her, as if inflated. Muriel Dosey is stooped, her hair dangling into the water, as if she were gazing at her own reflection, her hands placed across her breasts in what he feels to be an imploring gesture. Its meaning distracts him now as it distracted him then.

Another way to put it is that he is like a sock,

turned inside out. What is nearest his skin, he feels the least, what is distant he knows the best. Veiled by the dust raised by the cantering horse he sees the hands of his sisters waving to him from the buggy. They are on their way to church, with their father. He sits on the rear stoop of the porch or at the upstairs window, having refused to either ride to church or walk there. Soon enough, he refuses to ride, anywhere, with his God-fearing father. At seven years of age he walks three miles to school and three miles back. He is a child, but his stubborn will proves to be as inflexible as that of the father. This battle of wills will determine the course of his life. He will neither ask for help nor accept it when reluctantly offered. With the mother dead, he is like an unloved adopted child. As plainly as he saw the hands of his waving sisters—like ribbons blowing at the sides of the buggy —he sees that each of them, father and son, had effectively destroyed what they had loved. He sees that they each, if they had it to do over, would do it over again.

Would it be said that he was living, or merely seeing, parables? Leaving California, the morning sun in his eyes, he had sensed that he was traveling backward, but that the boy, in the seat at his side, at the same moment was hurrying forward, free as the wind. The same direction in space proved to be the opposite direction in time.

While the boy was there on the seat at his side, he could think of nothing that he wanted to tell him, although there were one or two things he might have told him, if he had been asked. All that he had not told, and not been asked, would end with himself. A film passed over his eyes as if a blast of cold air had chilled his face. He was relieved that the boy was not there to witness these involuntary shows of emotion, a sign, surely, of his weakened condition. He had long lived with the dread that one night he might wet his bed, or his pants. He understood from the complaints of others that something of this nature was not uncommon, although it was one of many things that exceeded his grasp. He had once watched the blood ooze from his arm, the result of a bullet he hadn't heard fired, his first experience with his body defying his inflexible will.

One thing he had meant to tell the boy was about the balls of fire. Seated on the padded board, across the arms of the barber chair (his head in a cloud of scented powder), he had heard the crash and the crackling like thunder, and blinked at the flash of light, like an explosion, opening wide his eyes to see the ball of fire that rolled like a hoop—he could see right through it—to where the road ended at the cattle loader, where it had popped, like a balloon bursting, the blades of straw, picked up as it rolled, driven like copper nails into the planks fencing the corral. "How come?" the boy would ask him. Electricity had done it. What it did, or might do, in those days was beyond belief.

Beyond the belief also (he now remembered) of some of those who had heard the story, and pointed out that if he had heard the explosion, which he did, it was after he saw the blinding flash, light traveling faster, even there in Chapman, than the noise it made. This obliged him to admit that what he had described was what he had *heard*, firsthand, from the barber, who had described it so well he had no need to see it himself. A boy's ears, his own especially, were often bigger than his eyes.

Was that why he had put off that story until he had been asked? Balls of fire, so common in the past, had grown so uncommon they might sound peculiar, or even downright stupid, to a boy who had watched a landing on the moon.

Had his sister Viola felt herself unraveling like a

ball of yarn? Or was this caused by the car, the riding, the ceaseless glide of the road coming toward him, slipping beneath him, and then on the instant (in the rear-view mirror) spilling out behind him. His feeling was that this movement added nothing to him, but carried something away. Surely Viola had been spared this humiliation, alone in her bed, shrinking all by herself. It was the old man's impression that his shadow had narrowed, as if drying as he looked at it. It also looked paler to him, as if cast by something that lacked substance. Nor could he keep track of the numberless ways the car seemed to unreel him, loosen his parts, shake him down to something less than he had been. Curled up in the trailer bunk he felt himself dwindling; he awakened from sleep to feel he had shrunk. In the washroom he did not glance up at the mirror until he was alone. The boy's knobby head impressed him as being larger than his own: a balloon full of air, as compared with one from which it had leaked, the skin wrinkled.

Had he dozed off at the wheel? He put his head to the window, into the whistle of a lark's song, certain that he had heard someone singing a hymn. Nothing is there. The telephone wires, on their tilted poles, rise and fall as they approach him. Some moments pass before he realizes the singing, the humming, had been himself, the last words of the hymn dry in his open mouth.

Brighten the corner where you are!

Hadn't he hated hymn singers all of his life? Or didn't that include hymns? A few moments of his life he had sat in a pew, his feet extended before him, listening to the choir and the throb of the organ. Before hymn singers there had been hymns. After almost eighty years of silence he remembered their verses. The way the past was coming toward him seemed to free him from the present and the future. He was no longer bound, as he had been, to his own life. The uncanny impression the day before, then his weightlessness in the circle of women, was not a fleeting sensation but his knowledge of the loss or gain of something. What gain could come from a loss of life?

He let the car coast to lift his hands from the vibrating wheel, and consider them closely. Hawks and Effie Mae had such talons. The fingers curled to form a rake. An injury of boyhood—a house jack had fallen to crush the first joint of two fingers—showed like the stitching of a glove seam. A doctor in Grand Island, where he had appeared to be drafted, put it down on the form as an "identifying scar." That had aroused him to the knowledge of his body as a place inhabited he would one day abandon. He had made much of that in a letter to Viola, citing the injured fingers, and the nature of the scar, so that no impostor, as he put it, might be mistaken for him in heaven. Just his letters to her were more than enough to see him in hell.

In the bunk of the trailer, his knees hugged to his chest, he would clasp the soles of his feet in his hands, holding himself like a wrapped package. Night by night, week by week, the contents of the package seemed lighter to him. From the sack of skin and bones something had evaporated: was it life? What he hugged in his arms was like a pod of dried seeds. His concern proved to be what he could clutch and hold to him. Skin and bones, the saddle-smooth soles of his feet. If the bedclothes had been thrown off his body he would have looked like a just-hatched bird. If dead, would he have been found clasped in his own arms? The thought of this so shamed him he tried to sleep in his customary manner, his legs stretched to lie one on the other, but they were so fleshless, the knees so bony, this actually proved to be painful.

Old man, this voice would ask him, what is on

your mind? Need he admit it? He felt that he owed it to his age, his weakened condition. So what was it? The womanly emotion of tenderness. This unmanly concern for his dwindling remains he felt with embarrassment and confusion. Had Viola been alive she would have been startled, and for once in her life unbelieving, that an emotion so frail, so womanly, had overcome his stubborn will.

THREE

In his periods of reflection the car might drift to the center of the road, and straddle the white line, as if it meant to relax. He fought this inclination, if he was not daydreaming, but the Maxwell had a will of its own. It, too, was old. It felt better, it felt safer, straddling the line. In Humboldt County, Kansas, there was not so much traffic that it proved to be a problem, unless he crested a grade. The Maxwell's speed was reduced on the grade to hover between twenty and thirty, so he didn't come on other cars as fast as they came on him. On the grade the motor tightened up, and ran quiet (it also ran a little hot on a long one), but on the downgrade the hammer of the loose rod could be distinguished from the general motor racket. The ideal condition was a speed of about thirty-five, against a slight headwind. The wind took up the slack in the motor and made it almost quiet in the cab, where the jolt of the wheel edging off the road was all that kept him awake.

If no one sneaked up behind him and honked, the Maxwell would slow down to the point it started bucking, and wake him up. He prided himself the way he could doze off and wake up just in time to keep the wheel out of the ditch grass. He couldn't do that with anybody's car: it had to be his own. Both east and west of Roswell the blacktop road was crossed by cattle barriers, made out of pipes or old rail ties, just wide enough that when the wheels hit them at about thirty-five it was like an electric shock: the vibration in his arms, the tingle in his legs, would last for miles. In the past, the dog would bark all the way to Alamogordo. The dog disliked the barriers, but what he couldn't seem to stand was to be held up at a crossing by a freight train. Did he think it was alive? Warner would have to whip him to shut him up. He lacked experience, that dog, he couldn't stand gas stations or the cough of a John Deere tractor engine, dislikes he may have picked up from Warner. All that muttering he often did under his breath was not lost on the dog.

Was there anything that dog liked? He liked a car with a real quiet idle. Warner could leave him in the car, and no trouble, if the motor had a quiet idle. The finest idling motor he had driven had been a Dodge five-passenger touring. What year? He had never given it much thought. The motor had what he would almost call a *ping*, like a good coin dropped on the counter. He might have been driving it now if his wife had not complained about the side curtains. He had been astonished. To his knowledge, until he married her, she had never ridden a mile in anything but a buggy. A mistake to have come up so fast? So he had thought. He had wooed her in a buggy, one that he had rented from the livery stable in Aurora, an advantage of the buggy—he had been led to reflect on it later—being the easy way the spring seat could be removed and carried through the cattail rushes to the river. She had asked no questions. It seemed to be acceptable to her for him to park the horse where it could graze on the ditch grass, or low-hanging willow branches, and go off with the buggy seat toward the river, but, later, if he stopped the *car* he had to leave the motor running, and let it run hot. "Muriel," he said, "I don't understand you!" It had made no impression on her. Perhaps it was the way she always said so little that led him on. Her nature was reluctant: one way or another, one place or another, seemed a matter of indifference to her, but in the matter of side curtains on the Dodge she drew the line. He traded it, in Amarillo, for the Maxwell coupe, never liked by the dog.

The blast of a horn, wind-borne toward him from the rear, led him to pull off the road and let the truck whoosh past, the suck of the wind stream lurching the cab. Up and down the rear of the trailer were the battered license plates of numerous states, like a patchwork quilt. A black exhaust plumed from the pipe at the front, drifting eastward on the prevailing wind. That hadn't changed. A wind like that infuriated him first, then ended up mystifying him silly. Why did it blow? His wife replied, "To turn the windmill, pump up water." The Indian in her found that perfectly sensible. Viola would have said, "God wills it," and both women would have exchanged glances, amused and baffled by the things that troubled men. When his wife took ill and lay awake at his side, resigned to illness, the wind and dying, the whir of the wind wheel, the clatter of the vanes as the wind veered or shifted, made him aware of a force in nature to match his own stubborn fury. This had led him (his wife dead, not there to turn her gaze on him) to let the wind simply batter the machine to pieces to be free of its ceaseless clatter. Was that accurate? He had believed it until this moment. Or had he, in this battle of wills, let the wind destroy a part of something bigger than he was? A visible reduction of the invisible forces he opposed?

From the bib of his overalls he slipped his watch, saw the face plainly, then put it away. For the *time* he cranked down the window and squinted at the overcast sky.

Why does that bring to mind the fire?

In the dusk of the yard he had watched the windows light up a moment, as if in a sunset, those on the first floor suddenly darkening as if with clouds. There was a pump right there at the door to the barn, with pails upside down on the corral fence posts, but it had never crossed his mind to put out the fire. Was there something inside he wanted burned up? Against the flames gusting out of one window he saw the hippie girl. He was struck by how much she looked like a stilt-legged boy. Feeling the heat of the fire (the sky was lit up with a shower of sparks), he turned to unhitch the car from the trailer, letting the hook-up drop in the yard with a thud. He got no

41

help from anybody—the boy had tailed off somewhere like a frightened rabbit—but the bearded hippie, without a rag on his body, lit up on the front as if he was half-roasted, stood holding his blue jeans watching the house burn. Ringed with fire, he looked like the devil personified.

It had been the old man's intent, no more, to move the old car back from the fire, out of range of the sparks, but the sight of Stanley put him in such a fury he headed down the driveway and just kept going. The way he hit the track crossing shook him silly, but didn't slow him up. Thinking he had come for help, and expecting him to stop, people gathered at the door and outside the café watched him go by. A fire hose cart had once been parked in the weeds beside the livery stable, but he had no recollection of an actual fire. This was an actual fire, and cast a flickering glow in the tops of the willows along the river. One sensible thing he did was slow down approaching the bridge. It had been of planks, the loose ones clapping like thunder, with a turnout near the center allowing buggies to pass. This half-mile-wide river (he had described it to the boy as not particularly deep, but a mile wide) appeared to be no more than a sandbar with pools of water too shallow to wade in. (Where, he wondered, had they baptized the women?) At the south end of the bridge, standing on the rail, he could see the peaked roof of the privy at the edge of the bluff. Gone? Willows screened it off. His father, his eyes on the horizon, had staked out his homestead on the bluffs, for the view. To enjoy it privately he faced the privy to the valley. His son often caught him there, his britches down, with *nobody to spy on him but God,* warming his knees in the sun. The fact that he had said that, and never tired of saying it, had always spoiled the view for Warner, both the summer and the winter prospect tainted with his monstrous love of God, and God's love of him.

Nevertheless he had been right about the view, and would have enjoyed the fire. It had been rumored of him, but never proved, that he had set his own haystacks on fire to watch them burn, like sinners in hell. Viola's house burned much better than a haystack, going up with a whoosh, once the roof caught, some of its heat borne on the breeze that rose off the river. The lights of the cars, focused on the smoke haze, made him think of a lynching witnessed by his father, but never described. It had made him more God-fearing than ever and an orator on the question of slavery. It shamed Floyd Warner, this man's only son, to hate him after eighty years as he had as a boy. "You're too much alike," Viola had said, "you both want something all to yourself." She didn't say God. There were always things she thought that she didn't say.

Except for the privy—at the edge of the bluff where the plowing left it undisturbed—nothing remained of the house and barns his father had built with his own hands. Back in the thirties, dust, blowing like smoke, had settled in drifts around the house like snow, burying tools and implements no longer of any use. A bulldozer had flattened the house and outbuildings to provide extra acres of rented pasture. What had not gone back to dust—including the nine in the cemetery—had now gone up in smoke. He found it strange the way his fury cooled with the fire, so he was able to gawk at it, like a neighbor. Car lights picked up the trailer, gleaming like a helmet, the enamel buckets on the posts fencing the corral, and nearer the fire, wavering like flames, the unmistakable figures of the boy and the hippie girl. Was it a trick of the light, the heat rising from the ashes forming streamers that flowed upward, that caused him to see her arms stretched over her head like a dancer? They lowered and raised, as if she stood there exercising. To his astonishment, he was able to see that she faced away from him, her back to the fire, observing the shadows her movements cast on the barn. He had forgotten her powers, the thralldom she cast over the boy. He had left the fire, he had driven to the bluff, and he had watched it all go up in smoke, not for one moment doubting that he would drive back when both he, and the fire, had cooled. Back to what? Had he reason to doubt all that he knew, as well as what he saw? Not only the house, not only the past, but the ties that had bound the boy to it, insofar as the boy was concerned, had gone up with the smoke. Nothing would be gained in going back, since there was, in truth, no place to go back to. He would not find in the ashes anything he valued, or what, until this moment, he had hoped to salvage, the boy being the one remnant of the past he had already lost.

Old man, so where are you?

He looks at the map. Kansas lies before him, a reassuring patchwork of straight lines and right angles. If he goes south, the west is on his right, the east on his left. Viola had written him of her concern when the center of the country, believed to be in Kearney, Nebraska (where she had attended the teachers college), was found to be instead near Osborne, Kansas, one hundred miles to the south. People living in Kearney, where everything was Mid-City, had to adjust themselves to the fact that they had never really been at the center of something, as they had thought they were. His answer to her had run to several pages—the vanity of man being one of his better subjects—with pointed asides as to what God would think of such fools made in His image. Actually, the news had put him in such a rage he had written to the postmaster general (the object and source of most of his complaints), asking who in the hell the government thought it was to make such a decision without consulting people, the center of anything being where they thought it was, until they were told or persuaded to think different. The center of a town was something people knew, and not something to be decided by a crew of surveyors, none of whom really knew their ass from a hole in the ground. He did not say that in so many words, but his intent was clear. Four or five weeks later he received a large packet of government bulletins, mailed without postage, on every subject except the one in question. As to where the center of the country was *now*, he couldn't care less.

One thing he would like to know—the car drifts to straddle the line in the road, as he thinks about it—is where the boy now is, where he will end up. It had seemed of small importance when it first crossed his mind—now he could not understand how it had happened. There had always been Viola to write and ask. There had always been a place. On the insurance card in his wallet he had written Floyd Warner, Chapman, Nebraska. There had always been a Warner in Chapman. The boy's name was Kermit Oelsligle. People wouldn't believe it even when they heard it. That he would never again hear it had not occurred to him. How was it possible to believe, to accept, something like that? Never hear it. Never really know where he was. All his long life the old man knew, and believed, that Viola's childish beliefs were impossible. Childish they were—but possible, graspable. Better the boy up in heaven, with Viola, than where he would never again set eyes on him, hear about him, or know where he was.

"For chrissakes, boy," he would say, "where you been?"

"Oh, around," he would answer.

"Around where?"

"Oh, just around."

The boy had a chipped tooth he swore he got biting himself. His claim was that he dived into the water then came up, too fast, under the diving board and thumped himself on it, biting himself so hard he had chipped his tooth. The old man never believed that for a moment, but he lacked experience in swimming pools. He had been careful to conceal the fact that he couldn't swim. It would not merely puzzle the boy to hear it, but discolor in a way that might disturb him the stories the old man had told him about the river. He would see it all different if all he saw him doing was *wading* in it.

He was startled by the appearance, right there at his window, of a freight locomotive pulling a caboose. It had come up behind him, without whistling, the track bed running along parallel with the road. The hulking monster put him in mind of some prehistoric creature, running for shelter. That was not so unheard of: creatures almost as large had roamed these plains before the ice age. Their bones had been found. They had lived so long ago his mind could not grasp it. The magnitude of such things had been pleasing to him in proportion to the torment they were to Viola, who found them contradictory to her faith. Without her to torment, or the boy to amaze, his pleasure in such vast prospects diminished. He cared less for monsters, more for the freshly painted Santa Fe caboose. It appeared to have been taken somewhere for a cleanup, the windows gleaming, the hardware blackened, the letters A.T.&S.F. bright as the raised lettering on a bank window. The dull sooty black of the freight locomotive made it look like new. In a caboose with three brakemen, two of them wearing the high-crowned denim hats, matching their overalls, Warner had ridden with his Uncle Verne from the junction at Columbus through the rolling sandhills to what his uncle's wife, Mae, described as a dirt farm. What other sort of farms were there? He had had the wisdom not to ask. Verne's wife—known as Great-Aunt Mae—had come from a non-dirt farm in Ohio, and took a superior attitude to farms deficient in cows and chickens. That in spite of the fact that half the chickens would blow off with the wind. A cow wouldn't, but there was little for a cow to eat. She kept cows, nevertheless, cranking the milk through a separator that might have been one of those on Viola's porch, the cream so thick it had to be spread on his oatmeal with a spoon. What had become of her? With Viola gone he no longer had anybody to ask. Warner had actually liked his Aunt Mae, but sensed that he should not, if he could help it, show it. Did she like him? "Let him stay another week," she said, "if he cares to." Why did she call her husband V.B. if his name was Verne? Years later he had grasped that calling him V.B. was a *sign* that she liked him. Likes and dislikes were largely a matter of signs. If Warner felt himself not actively *dis*liked, he understood that he was probably liked. Aunt Mae had no children of her own and frowned on the troubles one had with children, until they were able, as she put it, to help with the chores. Approaching the house with two full pails of water, the wire handles cutting into the palms of his hands, Warner had heard his Uncle Verne, looking up from the wash pan, his face glistening with water, say that one thing he could say was that the boy was not afraid of work.

"Is it something to be afraid of?" she had replied.

But he had sensed that it was. His uncle had implied it. His own nature at times rebelled against it. So the fact that he did it, without complaining, demonstrated that he was *not* afraid of it. Before he had left she would pour water for him into the pan his

Uncle Verne had just emptied, and he was free to use, like a hired hand, the other half of the towel placed on the drainboard, watching the letters come clear on the flour sack as it soaked up the water. Sometimes it proved to be sugar, instead of flour. He was *not* free, however, as Verne was, to toss his water into the yard through the screen bulge, but no one objected if he stood there with the towel and watched the hens scratch around the wet spot, or gazed out across the yard, booby-trapped with wire wickets left over from the previous summer when two of her nieces, who *were* afraid of work, played croquet for a week and then just left them in the yard to rust. They were city girls from near Zanesville, Ohio, and thought of nothing but boys.

At the top of a rise, white and looming as a lighthouse, a school building sat fifty yards or so back from the road. One side of the yard had been fenced, to keep in cattle, and the mesh of the fence was clogged with tumbleweed and paper blown there by the wind. At the back corners of the yard, equal distance from the schoolhouse, were two white privies with a chest-high wooden fence to screen off the doors. Through the film of chalky whitewash the old man could see the words stenciled on the boards: BOYS and GIRLS. A man who didn't *know* that, of course, might not *see* it, but he was experienced in such matters. Even more than experienced, he was at ease in such surroundings. Schoolkids. The empty yard suddenly alive with hooting and scrapping little monsters. That the bike rack in the side yard stood vacant meant that this was a holiday, or a weekend. He didn't know which. In either case he did not feel, as other strangers might, that in using the privy (so long as it was the BOYS) he was intruding or had an evil mind, waiting till the coast was clear to draw his own dirty pictures on the back of the door, or carve something on the seat. At the front of the yard there was also a pump, a tin cup dangling from a wire looped to the nozzle. Not to arouse the suspicion of local people (one thing they always knew was who was driving what car), he parked near the road and carried the canteen along with him. On the south side of the building there were two teeter-totters with splintered planks and well-polished seats. The nearer side was used as a playground, the windows protected by heavy cable screens. He noted with interest how the paint on the clapboards had been worn away by bouncing balls. Even around the pump not a blade of grass had survived the daily stampede. There was a caked mudhole, but no sensible seed would take root in it. It was a comfort to him to see it all, however, and imagine how it came to life at recess. In a wind like this they would never hear a whistle: he would have to ring a bell. Even the wind-swept yard, hard as concrete, provided him with familiar, friendly footing, the playgrounds and trailer parks of California being covered with acres of seamless blacktop. His dislike of kids, well known to everybody, did not extend to the school grounds in their absence. The vacant yard, the idle apparatus, pleased him with more than its unexpected silence. He had the impression of time arrested, of something lost, recovered. The swarm of faces, many new every year—he felt a weakness in his legs to contemplate it—dissolved away to this pattern he found reassuring. The faces changed. He clung to what resisted change in himself.

The wind blew on him in a way that made his feet seem light. He would first have a good pee, then he would have a long drink. Considering it was something he had never really liked (the wind puts a hand on his chest, to delay him, to give him time to reflect on it), how explain the way he had learned, for most of his life, to live with it? It might have been—once he stopped howling—the first sound recorded in his ears. It leaned on the house nine months of the year, leaving a disturbing hollow when it stopped. Even his mother said that if the house should fall it would be toward the wind, not with it, reeling over like a drunk whose support had shifted. He had grown accustomed, even as a child, to the siltlike talcum on the sills of the windows, where the tassels of the curtains, or the cord to the blinds, left tracks like small night creatures. One of the few things he had said to his father was that he was sick and tired of the goddam wind—the "goddam" thrown in to give it the predictable effect.

What had been the effect?

He delayed the pleasure of this reflection until he stood out of the wind in the privy. There were two holes; one for small bottoms, one for large ones. At the end of his life he was back where he had started, faced with the same choice. A strong eye-burning stench blew from the larger hole until he corked it with his bottom. It had the effect of increasing the quiet, as if a draft had been closed. The backside of the boards obstructing his view were scribbled over with verses, names, dirty drawings. At his eye level he read

Here I sit
Broken hearted

The next two and unforgettable lines (Warner knew them so well he needn't see them) had been boldly printed over with

NOBODY CARES

He was mystified why any snot-nosed farm kid, evil-minded by nature, would overlook the chance to repeat something dirty. Wasn't one reason for a privy to get off a kid's mind what he couldn't throw up? Did he mean to have a fourth line to rhyme with it, or just leave it like that? *Nobody cares.* It seemed a strange thing for a kid to write. It was more what an older, more experienced person might come to feel if he sat here for long, the door open, the plain empty and rolling as far as you can see it, the sky topless as far as you can feel it, the wind howling like a ghost in the uncovered hole at his side. Did Warner know about boys, having been one? Kermit Oelsligle would never believe it. With Warner's family of sisters, what boy had he known? Better than he cared to he knew Vance Fry, a boy so evil-minded he made a joke of it. Warner seldom saw him his beady little eyes were not squinted up tight, his lips smiling. He had the devil's cunning. His pockets were always stuffed with the Kewpie chalk he used to make dirty drawings. His father had been obliged to scrub off the sidewalks in front of the stores. How explain, in a boy of his age, what he could make of the words on the back of a tin of Prince Albert tobacco? With his knife—the mother-of-pearl handle in the shape of a woman's leg—he would scrape off words and letters so that what was left was slyly wicked. Try as Warner would, since he didn't believe in devils, he could only see it as a work of evil, not that of an eight-year-old boy. Vance had a small-size head, which didn't help matters, with his hair sticking up at the crown like a feather, his pants pockets weighted with marbles he had won playing keeps. He carried cinnamon oil in a perfume bottle, into which he dipped toothpicks, then sucked on them, which he said made the girls crazy to kiss him. What if it did?

Sheets of newspaper, cut into small squares, were spindled on a nail to the right of the door, but the type was too small for him to read. In his father's *out*-house—he did not like the word "backhouse," and frowned on the word "privy"—the previous year's Monkey Ward catalogue sat to the right of the holes, with a flatiron on it to keep the draft from flapping the pages. There were no scribblings on the door of *that* privy until farm hands, hired to help with the threshing, left it cluttered with drawings that had to be painted over before the father would let the rest of them use it. The girls walked the quarter mile to the Applegate farm, too small to need any hired help on it. These men were rough and foul-mouthed out in the field, but polite and respectful once they got to the table, yes-and-no ma'aming every move his sisters made. One of the younger men divulged to Warner what he did with his hard-earned threshing money. He went straight to Kansas City, where he got himself a good whore. He and this whore would get out of bed just long enough to eat, and they would stay in the bed until he ran out of money. He said he'd be glad to take Warner along with him, and "show him the ropes." This top and bottom side of men—he was a perfectly normal, good-looking young man when he was wielding a pitch-fork, or sat with his head bowed while his sisters said grace—flabbergasted more than it horrified Warner, since he did not at that time actually know what a whore was, good or bad. Sixty-five years later he still did not know. He had rebelled at his father's God and Viola's religion, but what was clean and unclean derived from their example, and nothing in his experience would make the flesh of such a woman desirable.

A gust of wind blew cool on his bottom, escaping

with a howl through the hole at his side. The wind along the Pecos, where he had taken his bride, howled like a creature trapped under the house. In the summer, up from Mexico, it blew hotter. In the winter it blew down from the snow-capped Rockies, lifting the sheepskins from the boards on the floor. You had to see it to believe it. Muriel never got over, being part Indian, the way the stove would howl like a coyote, the draft sucking up the flame so fast it would sometimes put the fire out. He had written to Viola that heathen superstitions seemed to him better founded than those she followed, and if he took it in mind to rise to heaven it would be on the draft up a stovepipe. She had not replied. It tickled him at the time, but shamed him now, that he had given his new dog the name of Jesus. "Why you suppose I call him that?" he had asked her. "The rabbit's good as dead till Jesus spots him, then he springs to life." When he had told that story to the boy he had just stood there, looking sheepish, which was one way he couldn't stand *anybody* to look. There was nothing dumber on this earth than a sheep, thousands of which he came to know personally, and he respected the good sense of Jesus Christ in referring to his followers in this manner.

So why raise sheep? He didn't like dirt farming. He couldn't stand being at the "mercy" of the weather. The farmer's stoical patience with the whims of nature, and his mutton-headed belief that "the Lord would provide," were equally repugnant to him. He didn't mind the sheep being dumb, if he himself was smart. He thought one man and a dog could handle a herd of sheep, and in the first winter blizzard he lost four hundred of them, packed like snow into a corner of the canyon. Even the dog lost track of them. Without moving a muscle, their heads all pointing into the corner, as if swimming, they had silently, mindlessly suffocated. Little more than three inches of snow had fallen, but it had been enough, with the wind blowing, to bury them alive. Cattle would do that, too, but at least it took more snow to cover them.

Not a wind sound, more of a hingelike creak rose from the hole at the moment he did, as if the seat had a squeak. Something shiny—anything and everything might be dropped into the hole of a privy—moved as if stirred by the wind. Again it squeaked. The match he struck, and held to the hole, the draft snuffed out. He made a wad of the newspaper, let it flare to a ball of fire, and dropped it. In the flood of light, eyes like bolt holes in a stove's hot belly returned his gaze. A rat? The eyes were too big. The body was multi-colored like a bread wrapper. All eyes and ears, what he had seen was a kitten, or what was left of a cat. It clung to the narrow two-by-four ledge that served as the privy foundation. If the boy had been there, the old man would have directed the operations. He would have held his legs, that is, while the boy stretched his arm into the hole. He was not there, however, and Warner stood a moment distracted by a fact to which he was not accustomed. It would have been a relief just to tell the boy what he should do. "You going to let a little stink be the death of that kitten?" The boy knew he didn't care much for cats. Now he kneeled to the floor, turning on his side so that his shoulder corked the hole, then reached to where his fingers closed on the knobby, furry head. A normal kitten would have clawed him good. This one did not. He drew from the hole such an object his impulse was to throw it back. It had been dropped —*dropped*—into the filth, and somehow managed to crawl up the wall to the ledge. Now that its eyes burned with light, it hissed at him, like a snake. He could bear neither to drop it nor to hold it, a tiny furry bundle of filth.

Naturally enough—he had to do something—he

left the privy and headed for the pump. It needed no priming: water spilled from the nozzle and he held the creature beneath it, like a dirty ball of yarn. The little fight left in it stiffened the body, but it was too feeble to claw him. The dousing gave it the look of a long-whiskered fish. He hustled to the car, wrapped the creature in a T-shirt—one with "Smokey the Bear" stamped on it—then placed it on the floor in the warm draft off the engine. Once the little mouth opened wide, like a feeding bird, but it made no sound. Did it mean to frighten him with just a look? The eyes lidded, the head nodded, as it tried to hold the fierce expression. "Sleep! Sleep," he said, matter-of-factly, and fluffed the material to keep the light out. Had he never before looked closely at a kitten? Foxlike ears. Inside one ants were crawling. The nose was pink, the faintest vapor at one nostril. What sex was it? He recalled that Viola preferred female cats. At the thought of her he experienced her outrage at what he knew had happened. Some goddam kid—the word "goddam" was invariably followed by "kid"—had brought a batch of kittens to school and another goddam kid had thought of dropping one down a privy hole. The vileness of man made his eyes film over, and aroused his fury against heaven. "Dear Viola," he would say, "I thought you should know what the good Lord is up to here in Kansas." He resented her dying, since he could no longer torment her with his letters. "You're such a stubborn old curmudgeon I just feel sure the Lord will have mercy on you!" What if that should prove true? Never in his life had he taken such nonsense seriously. But what about his death? He sat for some time, the cab rocking like a cradle in the wind stream of a cattle trailer, bits of straw and manure falling from the sky to ping on his windshield. Before starting up the car he glanced at the map to see where he was—to see where *they* were.

Garden City? On that previous trip they had stopped in Garden City to shoe the horse.

Under the spring seat of the buggy he had his own Gladstone, loaned to him by Wayne Wagstaff, a Burlington brakeman, and a fiberboard case, with straps, that contained her things and her *trousseau*. Where had she heard the word? It referred to garments that should never be worn. In those days she had been a girl with flesh so firm it took a good pair of teeth to bite her. With her dress over her head he was often tempted. Different than most women, she never squealed. One day into Texas a rattler struck her—a young one, almost too young to rattle. She had given him her hand, he almost fainting to see the blood spurt, where he had cut her, then shamed and mortified to feel desire for her as he sucked the wound. What sort of man was he? Like most, in her opinion. In the sand behind the house, some of it mixed with cement, he had taken her in broad daylight, while she strained to keep the laundry she was holding out of the dirt. He was something she learned to live with, like the weather, liking some of it, finding some of it irksome, but no cause for complaint. Was it the Indian in her? He had liked her being darker than his sallow sisters. She had a sentimental streak. If anybody said, "Have a good day, Muriel," she would make an effort to have one. Her older brother, Ivan, spent most of his time throwing his knife at trees.

Across the plains to the west, the tapering shaft of a grain elevator flashed like a mirror. On Mrs. Leidy's TV, in the trailer court, he had seen a moon rocket on its pad, waiting, smoking. "That's like an elevator!" he had exclaimed. She had never seen a grain elevator. He could not believe it. A woman from Pennsylvania, sixty-eight years of age. An elevator for her was one that went up and down, nothing more.

It didn't make her any younger, but she seemed as far removed from him as the boy.

At about the boy's age, maybe a year younger, he had been lifted from the street on the fourth of July to ride the same horse as Buffalo Bill, straddling the same saddle, his small hands gripping the horn. For a week his pecker had been sore, as if he'd rubbed it on the frame of a man's bicycle. That was something he had never told anybody, but he might have told the boy. He was not going to tell him anything he didn't want to know. When he began, "Now when I was a boy . . ." he could see him turn off. Did he think his Uncle Floyd had been somebody's uncle all of his life? The fact that he would always and forever be an uncle to the boy, plain and obvious as it was, was new to him. To the young, the old were born old, they came that way like old cars and old buildings. In the boy's mind that was how it was, and where *else* was he if not in the boy's mind? An old man with a trailer, a Maxwell coupe, and a sister, now dead, by the name of Viola. The youth Stanley had asked the boy, "Is that old fart your relation?" As he stood waiting for the boy's answer, Warner's eyes had watered. Would he ever answer? "Yeah," he had finally said, an admission forced from him by the need to tell the truth.

The strangeness of the fact that what he hadn't told the boy, the boy would now never know, made his limbs heavy. His hands keep their grasp on the wheel, but his foot slips from the gas pedal. Once more the car drifts to straddle the wavering center line.

What had he told him? That the way to clean a slate was to spit on it. "What's a slate?" the boy had replied. He hung around hippies and hippie places the way Warner had hung around gypsies. He is startled by how much they appear alike. The difference being that gypsies were gypsies, hippies were punks. What stories he might have told him—if he had been asked! These gypsies camped along the tracks, like hobos, and let their horses graze in the railroad ditch grass. They were known to be horse thieves. When the horses got old they sold them to glue factories, in Missouri. A kid of ten at the time, Warner would see their camp in the shadow of the railroad ties, west of town, or the glow of their fires under the water stack to the east. He had heard it rumored that they kidnapped white children only, and sold them for ransom, so he revealed himself, approaching so close they could see he was white by their own firelight, but nothing ever happened. Nor did he ever see them dancing. A woman nursing a child, dark as an Indian, came to the side of the buggy where Viola was sitting, rubbed the cloth of her skirt between her fingers, like money, then scuttled away. Viola would have given her the skirt if asked, but she was not asked. In the midst of a hailstorm he had seen some of the children running and hooting like little Indians, stooping to grab up a fistful of the hail and stuff it into their mouths. The boy, not knowing about gypsies, might easily think they were hippies. Their clothes were bizarre. They roamed about free as the wind.

If he had told the boy about these gypsies, their carefree ways, their adventurous lives, would he have been able to grasp that his Uncle Floyd had once been young? About this he felt a deeper injustice than he did about the two hippies. That had been his choice. But would he never understand that the old man, too, had once made one? Was it beyond him to grasp that Floyd Warner had once watched the big boys take their girls into the weeds behind the Chautauqua, and when they had left he would sneak in to lie on the still-warm trampled grass? He would never be told that. He would grow up and grow old without ever knowing how much, as *boys*, they were alike.

FOUR

Lulled by the idling motor, the kitten appeared to be asleep. How long since it had eaten? It might have been in that filth for several days. That led him to think of the cats back at the farm and who would now feed them with Viola gone. They lived in the barn. There might sometimes be as many as two dozen cats, half of them wild. It was not unusual for a person not to see them till the cows were milked, and they lined up to be fed. Once they got a whiff of warm milk their tails went up. Since he could remember Viola had insisted that fresh Guernsey milk was not good for kittens, unless they got it secondhand in the customary manner. It curdled in their stomachs, she said, or something like that. The old man didn't believe that for a moment, but he did feel that this kitten, after such an experience, should have something solid on its stomach. Mrs. Leidy, in the Rubio trailer court, fed her cat canned fish.

The tower of the grain elevator, now that he was getting closer, proved to be higher than he had imagined. The grove of trees at its base looked like bushes, the houses and freight cars like a toy village. It delighted him to see that this grain elevator had been recently painted, and the church hadn't. It stunned him to realize he no longer had Viola to torment with such observations. "There's this town in Kansas," he would have written, "where they got eleven churches and seven people. The folks are all so religious they just repainted the grain elevator." In recent letters he had kidded her more than usual to make sure she would write them right back, the boy being of an age he needed a good woman in his life.

The way the cab jolted crossing the tracks led him to stop the car and take a look at the kitten. He could see the light through one pink ear. A tiny spider moved about in the hairs, as if they were grass. A jumbled but appealing image of life within life, as small as this spider and as big as this earth, awed and instantly escaped him. In the river of his blood life swam. He had heard or read that somewhere. A woman known to Mrs. Leidy had once sat on a needle that turned up, years later, in her forearm, where it wanted out. It had traveled here and there in her body. She swore to it. That his own life had passed without his knowing about the life within him pleasantly dazed him. Over the Grand Canyon—so he had read—two huge planes had collided, having approached from opposite sides of the country, like two flies, a commentator had said, colliding in space. This awesome reverie was interrupted by the hiss of steam pluming to the left of the radiator cap. The column of red in the heat indicator pressed the flag at the top to signal *Danger*. Another time he might have instantly killed the motor. Now he let it run. He lifted the kitten from the floor—it seemed to be sleeping—and placed the bundle in the sun's rays on the shelf behind the seat, and as he entered the town of Minden Warner looked for a school building, which might have a water pump at the front or the back.

He bought gas in Minden, but rejected the suggestion that his fan belt needed changing. He had bought it new in California. The previous belt had lasted for eleven years. He did accept from the attendant a map of the Southwest, showing the roads to Roswell and south along the Pecos. At this time of year he could go in along the river, it would be so dry. Getting a buggy in and out was no problem, unless it was in the flood season, but once they had a car, which was not this one, getting in and out was often up to the car, there being no way he knew to keep the battery charged. After some months of experience he parked it on the rise halfway to the road, where a push might start it, but if the motor didn't catch it would set in the hollow until he got a horse to tow him, or a ride to where he could charge the battery. That car had been such a headache that when he did get it to Roswell he sold it for junk.

Across from the gas station a gleaming metal hitch bar ran the length of the street, the sidewalk shaded by a wooden awning. A horse was tied up at the hitch bar, a sight so unusual the old man considered it for a moment. A brown horse, nothing to speak of, with an army-type saddle over an Indian blanket. A young fellow of the type you only see in the movies, no shoes on his feet, a blue and white bandanna around his neck to keep his shirt clean, came toward the horse with a transistor radio held to his ear, like

70

it hurt him. "You want to buy a horse?" he shouted at Warner. Why did he think he would want to buy a horse? He got himself on the back of the horse, with some effort, and let it walk off with him as if he were wounded, holding his head. The music seemed to come from inside the horse.

Back in the shade of the awning a voice called out, "California? It wouldn't be Frisco?"

Until he said that Warner had forgotten the California plate. One of the things he had done in Chapman was wipe it off.

"It wouldn't *have* to be Frisco," said the speaker. "Salinas, Modesto, Bakersfield—you name it." The old man saw him dimly, back in the shade, until he came forward dragging an olive-green duffle. Above his reddish beard his face was the color of raw meat. Beside a pale, sallow man he might have looked healthy, his teeth gleaming when he smiled. Warner didn't like a man of his type in city clothes. The hoist he took in his pants revealed dirty feet without socks. Much as the old man disliked the young, in general, he disliked a canny old bum even worse. He had no sympathy for a man who would sleep in his clothes. This one was maybe twenty-five years Warner's junior, and from the way he acted he knew that. He resented Warner's having lived so long—never mind how he looked. The old man could judge that for himself in the way he was reflected in the café window. It was as if he sat on a stool at the counter, and had turned to look out. Behind him the street glared, so that his outline seemed to shimmer with a blue flame. He had always prided himself on being wiry. He had never before seen himself shriveled. What he saw was not a wiry old coot, but a shriveled old man. Back in Rubio, on the asphalt of the playground a child had printed

Mr. Warner is a potato bug

and he saw plainly as the nose on his face that the child was right. Buglike and bandy-legged, the head wider than the shoulders (the ears still growing), the hands dangling from the sleeves like roots. One would say that whatever he had been, the bug would out. It had not occurred to Warner, until he saw the reflection, that old men were impostors: inside they were one thing, but outside they were man-size potato bugs. This old bum with his duffle, who stood sizing up Warner, had not yet reached the stage of transformation. He looked like a people. Rolls of fat concealed the bug in him slowly emerging. He spit out the toothpick he had been chewing, prepared to come on strong with this stranger, this feeble old fart. "R-L-N?" he said, reading the letters off the license. "Now what county's that?"

Before Warner actually sensed what the issue was, he knew that it hung in balance. If he didn't call it, right off the bat, it would be too late. He thought of saying that it meant *Runs Like New*, which had been the boy's contribution, but it was not the best retort for a city-type bum like this one. "Owner's initials," he said, matter-of-factly, which was what the boy had wanted but they hadn't got, there being an extra charge for such nonsense. He dipped his head to pass beneath the hitch bar, then walked in the shade to the door of the café. A fan above the door blew the smell of chili into his face. A fly-specked mirror reflected the cook, who stood with his back to the counter, frying bacon. He was the nervous type who couldn't let a strip of bacon lie there and cook. The old man was crazy about hash-brown potatoes but not the ones that came frozen and they served half raw. He also had to keep in mind that he should eat something he could share with the cat. At one end of the counter a young man squeezed catsup from a plastic container onto a plate of French fries, and at the other a squat, broad-shouldered fellow leaned on the counter as he ate an ice cream cone. In the mirror behind the counter Warner saw his dark face, the hair, black as a crow's, that hung to his shoulders. He did not lift his eyes until he sensed that someone at his back was looking at him. A real Indian. Warner stood there, staring at him.

The cook said, "You don't have to sit at the counter, mister. There's tables if you don't care to sit at the counter." Did he think Warner was one of those people who wouldn't sit down to eat with an Indian? He seemed to. If Warner had been free to, he would have told the cook that the Indian's being there was no surprise to him. Quite the contrary. Seeing him there was almost reassuring. Of all the things in this world, or almost all of them, there was nothing that Warner disliked more than a day full of happenings like so many leaves blowing. Since morning, one thing had led to another, and they had all led to this seat at the counter. He returned the cook's stare. Behind the menu finger-painted on the mirror he could see the Indian licking the ice cream, his tongue smeared with the chocolate color.

"This fellow here," went on the cook—he had turned from the grill to point his flipper at the Indian

—"has been over there and come back. If you want to know what it's like, you should ask him." He put that question to the young man on Warner's right, who sat back on the stool in such a manner it pulled his pants far down on his buttocks, exposing patches of hair. Warner saw him through the eyes of the Indian. Clippers had worked around his ears and up the back of his neck, but below his ears he was a hippie.

"Man, I know what it's like." He gripped the bun he was eating with both hands to keep the slice of ham in it from slipping away from him.

"You know shit," said the cook. "You ever kill anybody? You ever see a man killed you just loaned money?"

"I ain't, and I don't plan to," said the young man.

To Warner the cook said, "Pop, what'll it be?"

"Two eggs, with hash browns," replied Warner.

The cook was relieved to have somebody as old and prejudiced as Warner to talk to. "Nobody knows till they been there, ain't that right, Pop?"

"Depends," he replied, "you been dead long, you don't know much."

The young man on Warner's right guffawed hoarsely, then choked up with a fit of coughing. No sound of any kind from the Indian. His attention was focused on doing one thing at a time. Warner knew about Indians, having once hired a boy by the name of Kira to herd sheep for him. He would spend days by himself on the open range. Warner had found the boy a slow learner but he didn't hold that against him. In those days the men would sell you the rings off their fingers, the blanket off their backs, if they had one. This Indian on his left had the smooth copper color of the one on the penny. On the right sleeve of his jacket he wore an emblem that looked newer than the jacket.

"What outfit's that one?" said the cook, giving Warner a wink. "The Cleveland Indians?"

Warner knew that was some sort of wisecrack, but he didn't get it. Were there Indians as far east as Cleveland? "You hear me?" said the cook. "What outfit's that one?" He moved to point his grill scraper at the emblem on the sleeve.

The Indian shrugged. "Not my jacket." He had nibbled the cone down to where he had to hold it between the tips of two fingers, like a cigarette butt.

"Not your jacket?" The cook saw he had a point there, but he decided not to make it. "I guess you guys get the surplus before we do, eh?"

Did the Indian hear that? Warner was thinking how the Pueblo-type Indians were a different kettle of fish from the Sioux and the Blackfeet, who lived in tents, and would as soon, or even sooner, kill a white man as look at him. This Pueblo-type Indian, a Navajo or a Hopi, turned on the stool to lick his fingers clean, like a cat. It reminded Warner of the one in the cab, and that he hadn't ordered food a sick kitten might eat. Getting no answer from the Indian, the cook had turned back to flip the eggs. "I've heard it both ways," he went on, to keep the conversation going. "If they don't like the war, they do like the girls. Ain't that right?"

The Indian raised his eyes to look right at Warner without seeing him. On the right side of his jacket, just below the shoulder, there were three small holes, one beside the other. They were brown around the edges as if they might have been burned with a cigarette.

"Ain't that right?" the cook repeated.

The young fellow on Warner's right replied, "If a booby trap blows it off, what good's a girl?"

"Hell," said the cook, "they'll sew you on a new one. They get a lot of spare parts in these wars, as well as jackets. You'll just never know what you'll find in war surplus till you go and look!" He slapped his flipper on the grill, then added, "Never mind how you like it, buster, just be glad you're back!"

"Why be glad am back?" replied the Indian. The cook had not expected him to answer that one. The old man was thinking there was nothing you could say to which somebody wouldn't take exception.

"Hell, you're alive," said the cook. "You're not in a goddam box." Having said it, he seemed to wish that he hadn't, but the Indian let it pass. "Nothing's perfect," said the cook, "but the killing's over—"

"What killing over?" answered the Indian. He showed no emotion. He asked as if he was ignorant, and wanted to know. From the napkin dispenser he removed one of the napkins and carefully cleaned his sticky fingers. The calm way he did it led Warner to feel he missed the gist of the cook's statement.

The cook said, "You know what that napkin cost me? You're free to use it, but you know what it cost me?"

"No," said the Indian. "What it cost you?"

The old man couldn't figure out if it was what he said, or something in his manner. The cook said, "Let's forget the napkin. Let's just you and me forget the goddam napkin, no matter what it cost. Let me just ask you what it costs me to provide you with a

stool for your ass to sit on while you sit and eat a
fifteen-cent order. You know what my time is sup-
posed to be worth? Let me ask you that."

The Indian had been served a glass of water. They
watched him take two little swallows of it. Someone
like the cook might be led to think that he had merely
spoiled it for anybody else. To cool things off Warner
said to the Indian, "Young man, what is your name?"

"George Blackbird," he replied. "Old man, what is
yours?"

Warner was too flabbergasted to be offended. Did
he mean to be like that, or didn't he know better?

"Blackbird?" said the cook. "That's translated from
the Indian?"

The slow movement of his head seemed to be an
assent. It took time, the old man was thinking, to get
accustomed to their impassive manner.

"My name's Warner," he said, since he had been
asked. "Floyd Warner."

The cook said, "Why you Indians so strong on the
bird idea? Blackbird, Thunderbird, Warbird, so
forth?"

"What's wrong with that?" said the young man.
He took a swallow of his Coke. "I like it better than
Clay, which is the name of dirt."

"Your name is Clay?"

"Clay's my first name. Another thing is, they often think it's my last name."

"It wouldn't be Clay Ridge?" asked the cook. He winked at Warner, assuming the Indian wouldn't get it.

"No, it wouldn't," the young man replied. He didn't say what it would be.

"Old man," said George Blackbird, "what you want?"

In the pause that followed they could hear the bacon frying. Warner really wasn't sure he had heard it right, or if it was something he had sat there thinking, having heard it before.

"His name is Warner, like he said," the cook retorted. "He'd probably like a cup of coffee, for one thing. How about a piece of pie?" He moved to one side so Warner could see the pie in the case. It was all pie with the meringue piled on it to look like a cake. It hadn't crossed his mind that the Indian thought he wanted more to eat. "I see you're driving," said the cook. "Which way you headed?"

"West," he replied. "Just east of Roswell."

"What's there to do in that country?" asked the cook. "You in cattle?" The old man sensed he didn't care a damn, but did it just to keep the Indian from talking.

"Sheep," he replied. "I'm a sheep rancher."

"God bless and protect you!" said the cook. He shook his head in the manner of a man well known to sheep. "I've seen more people lose their shirts in sheep—"

"Well, I didn't lose mine." It made him conscious of the old one he had on; he hadn't changed it in weeks.

"You were either smart, or you were lucky. The only sheep I like is a lamb chop."

Warner restrained his impulse to point out that lamb was not sheep. A man that dumb was not a man to discuss the sheep business with further.

"I wasn't so smart. I just did it by myself. Me and the dog."

"I'm interested to hear you say that," said the cook. "You must be about the last white man in the business. I understand they brought in these Basques, from Europe, when they couldn't get Americans to do it. They go off and live on the range with them, for weeks at a time."

"I lived with them"—he couldn't help but say it—"day in and day out for seventeen years." He saw that the cook didn't believe it. "Then I gave it up and moved to California."

"So why you go back?" said George Blackbird.

The cook said, "You previously asked this gentleman what it was he wanted. I'd say what he'd like is to be left alone to eat, to finish his meal in peace."

The old man might have left it there, but he thought it curious for the Indian to ask him what he was asking himself. "I was just visiting my people, along the Platte. On the way back I thought I'd look in on the homestead."

"Was what you had a homestead?"

"Yes, sir, that was what I had." It pleased Warner to speak to someone who could appreciate a homestead. So far as he knew it wasn't yet of much value, but one day anything fronting on the highway would be. The way people were coming, they would crowd into hell once they opened it up.

The cook said, "You rent it out or sell it?"

"I let it set," he replied, and that's how he saw it on his mind's eye. The cabin sitting on the rise, not a good place for it, down in the hollow would have been better, but it was what Muriel wanted and what she got. Up there she could see to the Rockies in the winter, or turn and look along the Pecos in the spring and summer, the water as green as the willows until muddied with the rains. A nice place except for the goddam everlasting wind. "It sets back—" he said, waving his hand to the left, "not much on it but the cabin."

"How's it for fish?" said the cook. "Maybe I'll rent it. God, do I love to fish!"

Truth to tell, the old man didn't really know, not caring for fish. There were fish in the Pecos when there was water, but right now there would be little water.

"You go there now?" George Blackbird asked. Even the cook thought the question more respectful. Blackbird leaned on the counter, folding the napkin he had used into an airplane. He held it up as if he meant to sail it, then changed his mind.

"I'm thinking of just looking in," Warner said.

George Blackbird nodded. "Me, too."

What did he mean by that? What he meant, it turned out, was that he was just looking in on his own people, who were near Winslow.

"That mean they're Hopis?" asked the cook.

That wasn't what he meant, but it was what they were.

"I was a cook for two winters at the Thunderbird Lodge up at the Canyon," said the cook. "I got to know a lot of Hopis." He extended toward the old man the ring finger on his right hand. An uneven piece of turquoise, darker at the edges, was set in silver framed by six silver drops. "That's a real one, Pop. One of the old ones. The drops stand for rain. The turquoise in their language stands for the sky."

They all waited for George Blackbird to comment. The ring was there for him to see, but he ignored it. "I happen to *know* this is an old ring," said the cook. "The Indian put it in hock. They gave him twenty bucks for it. They don't give you twenty bucks for anything that's not old."

A cool draft of fresh air blew George Blackbird's paper airplane from the counter to the floor, where he let it lie. The cook looked to the door and said, "You're welcome to step in or step out, mister." In the mirror behind the counter Warner could see the bum with his olive-green duffle, framed in the door. He couldn't seem to make up his mind to step in, or back out.

"I don't mind waitin'," he said, "if I know I got a ride. You plan to move along soon?"

"Don't rush a man when he's eatin'," said the cook. "For chrissakes, nobody likes to be rushed. Let the man have his coffee."

"No rush," said the bum, "I just need to know if I got a ride." He put a smile on his face that made him look like Happy Hooligan in the mirror. Warner didn't speak. He let the cook add hot coffee to his cup. George Blackbird rose from his stool as if he meant to leave, and the bum at the door stepped out to let him pass. Instead of stepping out, he closed the door in the bum's face. The cook couldn't believe it. The bum couldn't believe it. George Blackbird stood there, his hands in his jacket pockets, so that the coat hugged him at the hips. Near the middle of the back, like buttons, were four bullet-size holes. Warner was thinking that the way they did things today it might have been only yesterday he was at war, somewhere in Vietnam.

"Bygod, you do beat all," said the cook. "You learn that in the Army?"

George Blackbird remained facing the door, returning the gaze of the man he could see through it. The bum looked more dumbfounded than mad. He wouldn't know what to think until something else happened. "The nerve of that old bastard," said the cook. "I wouldn't give him the time, if I were you. I'd let him walk."

George Blackbird's head nodded. "He walk—I ride."

It was neither a question nor an assertion. In either

case, it was not what Warner was accustomed to deal with.

"Wouldn't you say that was up to Mr. Warner?" asked the cook. George Blackbird didn't say who it was up to. The cook would have preferred, the old man would have preferred, and even the young man, Clay, would have liked it better if he had turned from the door and faced the mirror, instead of showing them his back. Seeing only his back in the mirror led them all to turn and look to the front. The bum had moved from the door to lean his duffle on the front fender of the Maxwell.

"Unless I need someone to spell me off," said the cook, "I personally like to travel by myself. People got their own habits. Most of them either talk or they smoke too much. I picked up a kid west of Topeka who played the mouth organ all the way to Garden City, where I let him off."

One thing about Indians, Warner was thinking, was that they didn't talk much. In his first year on the ranch he had a boy named Awa help him with the sheep. He was pretty good with the sheep, and almost cheap as a dog. He disliked coffee. He didn't like water on his hands or face. Muriel couldn't understand until she asked herself how he lived in that wind without his skin cracking. The dust on his skin was like a talcum, until he washed it off. It was hard for them both to get over feeling dirty and settle for one or two baths a winter, but that was the way to get through the winter without their hands and wrists cracking with the chap. That little Indian could live in the wind like a bird. The only trouble they had was that there was no way to tell a dumb Indian from a smart one, both Indians being short on talk. Warner had given the boy a board and set of checkers for Christmas but later found he had used them as wheels to make toys and skates. Was that dumb or smart? If he had to go somewhere in a car, however, and choose between a white bum and a dumb Indian . . . "Mr. Blackbird," he said, "where you headed?" The Indian sat there as if wondering. "I'm not going so far today," the old man said, "but I'll take you as far as I go."

Did Blackbird think that was reasonable? He still didn't say. He did turn to look at a rack of Hostess cupcakes and select a pack with the chocolate icing. As he accepted his money the cook said, "I ought to charge you extra for the napkin, you know that?"

Clay said, "Which would you rather have, napkins or trees?"

"You ever wipe your ass with a tree?" asked the cook. The old man had, as a matter of fact, but he was not fool enough to admit it. To the Indian the cook said, "You travel light, I will say that."

Blackbird paid for the cupcakes with pennies, stacking them in little piles of five on the counter. He helped himself to a toothpick as the cook rang up the sum.

Warner said, "You wouldn't have some scraps for a cat?"

"They won't eat scraps. That's why I don't have one. You got a cat that eats scraps you got something special." He wagged his grill scraper at the cans of tuna arranged in a pyramid behind the counter. "That's what they feed cats now," he said. "I've seen it on the TV."

George Blackbird said, "Cats eat fish. Like fish."

"How much a can of that worth?" the old man asked.

"Cost me thirty-eight cents wholesale. It's worth forty-five to me; what's it worth to you?"

The old man was thinking how he used to buy fish, maybe it wasn't tuna, for nine cents a can. That was fish for himself. "I'll take one can," he said, then he added, "I'll never get it open. You got an opener?"

"This is a diner," said the cook, "not a goddam dime store."

"I just mean to open it," Warner replied. The cook put the can on his cutting board, then used an old-fashioned opener to cut it open, leaving the crimped-edged lid still attached to the can.

"Don't cut yourself when you pry it up. There's nothing sharper than a goddam can lid."

"Blade of grass sharp, too," said Blackbird.

In another situation Warner might have said, "You're one smart Indian!" but in this one he didn't. What he did was stand a moment looking at him. Would anyone but an Indian know about the edge on a blade of grass? Holding the can by the rim, careful not to tip it—there's nothing that lasts so long on your fingers as fish oil—he walked out through the door the Indian held open to the cool shade of the awning, the fan blowing at his back. Then he let the Indian lead him to the car, as if he might need help getting the door open. The old bum had his duffle between the hood and the fender, as if that was his customary place to store it, but George Blackbird, as if he did it all the time, as easy as a postman handling a mail sack, picked it up by the drawstrings and gave it a swing over the hitch bar to where it plopped on the walk under the awning. He did it so easy anybody would have said it was Blackbird's car. He opened the door for Warner to climb in—first leaning in to put the can of tuna on the back shelf—then he walked around the car to let himself in the door on the other side. That was the door that might open anytime, and the old man kept it wired. "Hold on," Warner said, and leaned over to unhook the coat hanger from the handle. Blackbird let himself in, then wired it up as if it were something to which he was accustomed. A really smart Indian. Was it the war that made him so smart? Warner almost felt grateful toward him for getting him out of a sorry situation with the old bum. He had a chew in his mouth—Warner could see it, the way he stood staring with his mouth open—and would have spent his time cranking the window up and down so he could spit. A smart Indian like Blackbird might smoke a little, but he wouldn't talk. In choosing a red man over a white man—and he didn't really choose him, he had been chosen—Warner felt less guilt than he might have since most people impressed him as no damn good, especially whites. Another thing about Blackbird, the moment he got in the car he didn't peer around and make smart cracks about it, or ask if it was a wood or coal burner. To an Indian a car was a car. One thing Warner would have done, if alone, would have been to see where he was on the map, but he didn't want to give Blackbird the idea he had to look at a map to see where he was going. The Maxwell bucked a bit when he put it in reverse, so that the canteen dangling from the choke handle thumped Blackbird on the shin. Without asking if he might, the Indian shortened the strap so that it wouldn't swing, unscrewed the cap and took a swallow of the water, put the cap back on, then sat with it propped between his thighs. How long was it that Warner, a foolish smile on his face, just stood or sat and watched such things happen? It seemed to him, since morning, they were watched by something in him besides himself.

Since Muriel had died, and he had gone looking for another wife, Warner had not sat this close to an Indian. On his way to California he had stopped in Gallup, where the all-night diner had been full of them. When he came out of the diner, unaccustomed to the traffic, he had been hit by a pickup without any headlights, three ribs broken and his leg sprained. The nurse who looked after him had been a young lady from Pasadena, named Eileen Coyle. She had come from California to put in a year of practical training among the Indians. She did not like the soft life of Pasadena. She loved the life of Indians on the reservation. In less time than it took for his leg to heal he had asked her to marry him, and she had accepted. She did not like many white men in general, but she liked him. Warner was not experienced in judging young women, and she was inexperienced in judging older sheep ranchers, believing right up to the moment they left the highway, east of Roswell, that he was taking her back to one of those Rancho Grandes, with a big hacienda, she had seen in the movies. They came in after dark so she didn't see much, but it had been enough.

Sometime toward morning, while Warner slept, she hiked back to the highway and got a ride somewhere. She never wrote to him, nor returned for her three suitcases full of clothes. A lawyer in Santa Barbara later notified him that the marriage had been annulled. To think about it now, almost thirty-five years later, left him as speechless as it had then. A woman old enough to flirt with him, to marry him, to give up, as she said, her career for him, had refused to get out of the car when she saw the house in the flickering headlights. Her expression had been that of a woman too startled to scream. He couldn't budge her—she had been a girl on the hefty side, almost as tall as he was—so he had left a lamp burning so she could find her way when "she came to her senses." Whatever senses she had come to had led her to climb out and take off.

Thanks to this young woman—Warner no longer had, if he ever had, a clear picture of her features—his appreciation of the woman he had married came too late. Muriel Dosey's only complaints had been about the flapping side curtains of their first car. She would rather walk, she said, but she meant that as a simple statement of fact, not a threat.

As if he smelled something burning, Blackbird tilted his head back and sniffed the air. The sun on the cab had made it hot.

"It's the fish," Warner explained, since he could smell it himself. But Blackbird knew the smell of canned fish, and that was not it. He bent over low to sniff the air under the dashboard, as if it might be something wrong with the motor. Warner let the car drift and the motor idle: a good nose might save them both a lot of trouble. But what Blackbird smelled was not under the hood but in the hot air of the cab: he turned to sniff behind him. On the shelf

at his back his gaze fastened on the soiled Smokey
the Bear T-shirt. At one end of it the kitten's ratlike
tail was visible. Blackbird moved his head closer,
then drew back as if he didn't like cats, his lips
pressed together.

"It's asleep," said Warner. "I'm letting it sleep."

Did Blackbird doubt that? He turned in the seat
once more to sniff the air, then gripped the tip of the
tail, the T-shirt falling away as he held up the soiled
lifeless body. Blackbird looked directly at all there
was to see, then flicked it, like a match, through the
lowered window.

"Dead cat," he pronounced, "more surplus."

Why didn't Warner speak up? He had gone to
considerable trouble to salvage the creature, and how
could he be sure that it was dead? Did Blackbird see
things more clearly? Could he be sure of Blackbird,
if not himself? The Indian's attention had been
diverted from the cat to the opened can of tuna on
the same shelf. He picked it up, careful not to spill
the oil, using the nail of one finger to pry up the lid,
placed it on the seat between them, then tilted to one
side to search in his pockets for a knife. With the
small blade of the knife he speared hunks of the tuna,
carried them to his mouth. Was that, too, something

94

he had learned in the Army? He ate about half the tin, then pressed the lid flat on what remained, cleaning the blade of the knife on the leather of his boot top. Naturally he was thirsty, after eating the fish, and had himself several swallows from the canteen, leaving a film of fish oil from his lips on the spout.

The sun shining through the windshield increased the heat in the cab, and the smell of the fish. Into Warner's head, out of nowhere, popped a notion so strange it made him smile. The moment coming up, the one that came toward him like the line on the highway, then receded behind him, was something he had no control over. He could watch it coming, he could see it receding, but he could do nothing to avoid it. The Indian, the cat, and the prayer ceremony had come out of nowhere to take him somewhere. He could see it happening. He could see that it was not an accident. He had come this way by his own free choosing, and having chosen as he pleased, he was right where he was. One thing led to another, to another, to another, like the count of the poles that passed his window.

"What you say?" asked Blackbird.

Had Warner said something, or did the fellow hear what he had been thinking? He was one smart Indian.

Warner didn't like him, but he paid him his respects. Now that they were driving west the lowering sun made Blackbird squint as if he was smiling, but Warner knew it was more of a grimace, as if salt burned his eyes. Now long accustomed to it, neither of them noticed the smell of the fish.

FIVE

Sometime later he woke up with Blackbird wrestling him for the steering wheel. The left front wheel of the car was sweeping the ditch grass on the wrong side of the road. Fortunately Blackbird, who proved to be stronger, forced the wheel in the other direction. "What in the goddam hell!" the old man shouted, too worked up and startled to keep his mouth shut.

"You fall asleep," said Blackbird, "drive off the road."

Warner could not deny it. The truth was he was accustomed to being spelled off, especially late in the day.

"Old man, I drive," Blackbird stated, and Warner could think of nothing to say. Blackbird seemed in no hurry, taking time to pee in the car's cool shade when Warner stopped it. He also seemed familiar with the principle of the gear shift, but he was not so adept at it as the boy. The car bucked and died. On starting up again, he almost shifted into reverse. The changeover had loosened them both up a little, and Blackbird helped himself to one of his cupcakes; the old man declined. By way of explanation, not to hurt his feelings, he explained that he didn't like to eat without his coffee, especially anything sweet. He would often as not go without eating rather than eat then find he had no coffee.

Blackbird said, "You like me, you got no people."

Actually, Warner had said nothing much about people. The Indian always seemed to infer more than Warner had said. "I've got people," he said, "here and there, but no more in this part of the country. That's what brought me back."

"No people is bad," said Blackbird.

In most respects the old man would deny that, having lived most of his life without them, but he understood that Indians were of a more sociable nature. It was enough for them to be around each other. They didn't have to talk. "What became of yours?" Warner asked him. Blackbird shrugged. The old man was sure he meant to go on, if for no other reason than he had been asked. "Not only Indian people have a bad time," he continued, "it's a bad time for people in general. Families break up. They move around too much. They don't have their own place."

"Indians move around, too," said Blackbird, "move around to hunt, to fish, to kill."

The old man was made ill at ease by the word "kill." It was the Indian's nature to speak like that, but in the context of their talk the word was disturbing. Why couldn't he have said to hunt and to fish, and let the matter drop?

"I suppose that's true," Warner replied, "but you still don't move around as much as we do. Pueblo people stay put, most Hopis and Navajos stay put."

"No stay put," said Blackbird. "Keep put."

The old man had to respect a smart Indian. He tried to catch his eye in the rear-view mirror, but Blackbird kept his narrow gaze on the road. "I suppose that's true," Warner added.

"Keep put till killing," Blackbird said, "then draft him."

If he wanted to refer to the war as the killing, Warner was not prepared to argue with him. It did seem he used the word more than he had to. Did he use it because he liked it?

"The killing is bad," replied Warner, to put

Blackbird at his ease. He wagged his head as if to free it from the thought of the pointless killing, the millions who were now dead.

Blackbird also shook his head, then said, "Killing not bad—always killing something."

Warner gave himself time to think over what he had heard. There were good wars and bad wars, as everybody knew, but he would not refer to wars as good or bad killings. An Indian might. In that respect, among others, he was different from a white man. It amused the old man to see an Indian like Blackbird in a white man's war, the issues simplified to killing or being killed. Warner knew Indians, he had hired them, he took it for granted they weren't like white men, so his feeling about Blackbird's withdrawal was not a personal matter: no better or worse than that of a stranger asleep in a bus seat. This would not, however, explain Warner's feelings when Blackbird took the trouble to look at him. His small black eyes were without expression. He did not wink or blink or move his head to indicate he was being looked at. If he had been a dog, he would not have wagged his tail. When the cat had stopped hissing at Warner like a snake, he had looked at him in a similar manner. Impersonal. Nobody knew, for sure, what was on an Indian's mind, least of all, maybe, an Indian, but Warner had not previously felt how little it mattered. There sat Blackbird. Here sat Warner. The poles made a sound as they passed the car window.

"Always killing something," George Blackbird repeated. Then he added, "My father kill his younger brother."

Not to show shock—Blackbird showed none—the old man said, "A family quarrel? They had a fight over something?"

"No quarrel," said Blackbird. "According to tradition, older brother kill younger brother." The old man did not speak. He did not feel, as he should have felt, a rising flood of anger; he felt only tired. Blackbird was a presence, Blackbird was a force, outside of his experience. He was like the boy Stanley and the girl Joy: he was too much. "No traditions now," continued Blackbird, "less killing. Older brother in jail now for killing. For an accident."

"An accident?" Warner echoed. He was not sure he cared to hear about it.

"My brother, four braves, go on raiding party. They ride three days into enemy country, raid tent of enemy braves, make many blows on him. Then my brother make a blow, but by accident kill him.

101

A good raid, with good blows, but he kills by accident. They find and put him in jail. For killing by accident they put him on trial."

It was a long speech for George Blackbird; now and then he raised both hands from the wheel, the palms forward. There was something to be said about the white man's justice, but the old man could not say it. His wits seemed dazed, as if the *words* had been blows. In a similar situation—that one, too, in the car—the young hippie Stanley had said something that had outraged him. But he had said nothing. He had done nothing. He had not relieved himself with a stream of curses. He had been faced with something with which he could not *cope*, a word he had picked up from the hippies. He had failed to cope then, and he failed to cope now. In a Reno washroom, as he stood buttoning his pants, he had heard one of the men in the booths telling a story, he did not know to whom. The gist of the story was that a woman being raped, if she was smart, would relax and enjoy it. He couldn't cope with that either, but perhaps his resignation was of that order. Did a woman after rape feel as he felt?

Slouched in the seat, Warner alternately dozed and watched the blood-red horizon darken, indifferent to the fact that this meant tomorrow would be a good day. Now and then lights came toward them like puffballs shot from Roman candles, exploding as they struck the windshield. He had been asleep when they stopped at a red light, and a car heavily thumped the rear bumper. A pickup truck, crowded with young hoodlums, honked to attract Blackbird's attention. The old man was relieved it was the Indian at the wheel, not himself. They drew alongside, leaning out to leer at them, howling their obscene remarks at the Maxwell. Only days before, Warner would have cranked down the window and cursed them silent. The young were amazed to see such fury in an old man. Now he observed them with a curious detachment, as if their speech were alien to him. Blackbird parked the car at the side of a diner where the windows were lit up. Warner might have been a child, on a railroad platform, peering up at the lights of a diner, but now he looked without envy, without wonder, without appetite.

Did Blackbird assume he was asleep? As if he thought the old man might drive off and leave him, he took the keys from the ignition, then walked through the diner to the men's room at the back. Before he came back to a seat at the counter, Warner had dozed off.

During the night, the car moving, he awoke thinking he was riding in the trailer. That was not un-usual, but he could not carry the thought through to its conclusion. Who was driving? Where were they going? He went on musing without knowing. On a rise, somewhere, he opened his eyes to see what he thought was the farm burning, but it was only the lights of a town reflected on the clouds.

SIX

Where were they?

A film of rust-colored water splattered the windshield, the light coming through the window at the back of the cab. The glare was so direct the old man thought it might be the light of an approaching locomotive. It was the sun, however, looking like an explosion in space. With blinking eyes, he seemed to wait for the report. Out here where distances were hard to judge he had learned to estimate them the best he could, noting the length of the gap between the flash of lightning and the peal of the thunder. That storm's about forty miles away, he'd say to Muriel, and often it was.

No one sat at the wheel; the cab door hung open to show the hard, cracked surface of mud in the ditch. On the far side of the ditch was a tilted pole with a single glass insulator on a peg at the top. The sun had faded its bright bottle-green color to that of smoked glass. It no longer bore a wire, so the pole would not hum if a boy pressed his cheek, or an ear, to it. Even in the old days he had had trouble with the men who used the glass insulators for target practice, turning off the power that pumped his water. In the spring, when the Pecos ran clear, he often carried water to the house in milk cans. Every drop of rain dripped into gutters that carried it to oil barrels for storage. When the level of the water was low there might be tadpoles swimming in the dipper. Muriel refused to drink it. She feared they might swim forever in her insides, or turn into frogs. Had living out here shortened her life? The doctor in Roswell had made no comment. "I wouldn't say her life was easy," Warner had said, thinking the doctor might contradict him. But he did not. "No, I suppose not," he had replied. No woman had an easy life on a homestead, but they had never lacked for essentials. Nor had it been for the lack of money they went without luxuries. To bring a privy into the house had always impressed her as foolish. If it had been there, she might have paid money to get it out.

They had both thought, when they were older, to get a little farm in Oregon, with some trees on it, with a woods nearby where he could hunt and fish. "I don't feel right in my side, Floyd," she had said, and two weeks later she was dead.

Would the Indian have said something *killed* her? Through a hole between splatters Warner could see him pouring water into the radiator. A vapor of steam slowly appeared, but did not blow off. The way the Indian was darkened by the cab's shadow, the old man felt it might be evening. What time was it? The moment he asked he knew where he was. The sun came up like that to warm the east wall of the house till the boards creaked, like branches, warm to his hand while his breath smoked white in the darkened room. It did not seem remarkable the car had stopped where it did, but merely the last in a series of inevitable events. One thing led to another. No accidents.

"What happened?" he called to Blackbird.

"Motor run hot. No fan belt."

If I were you, the man in the station said to Warner, *I'd change this belt*. But the man was not him. He was a man called Tex by the boy at the pumps. Warner unhooked the coat hanger from the handle of the door and pushed it open so he could climb out. For a moment he stood beside the car, unable to straighten up. Blackbird moved to look at him. "Old man, you sick?"

He was old, not sick. He asked, "Where we at?"

One hand shading his eyes, the Indian stared down the road to the east, as if he saw something. A moment passed before Warner saw the girders of the bridge, as if slowly approaching. They were painted white. He could not recall a white-painted bridge.

"Pecos River," said Blackbird.

On the hills around him Warner saw the sparse growth that only a fool would have tried to graze sheep on. A man like himself. Not to question what river it was, he said, "I don't recall the white bridge."

"Painted white," said Blackbird, "so drunken Indian see it better at night."

"If that's the Pecos," said Warner, "we can let the car set. The road to my place turns off just beyond it. I can let it set till I get into Roswell, get a new belt."

George Blackbird had raised both sides of the hood so the motor could cool; he stood gazing at it. Warner recalled how the Indian boy Awa would marvel at the Dodge and feared to crank it. In his

Indian mind that made it come alive, and dangerous. Blackbird knew about cars, but he was still an Indian and perhaps he also marveled at what made it run. Like an animal it needed water when it ran hot.

"One thing about the road through here, Mr. Blackbird, is that there's a lot of traffic on it. It's a main route. You'll have no trouble getting a ride." Warner felt he couldn't make it much plainer than that, that this was the end of the road, for them both. He leaned back into the cab for the ignition keys, the flashlight behind the seat, and the canteen. A half carton of Fig Newtons, left by the boy, was stored under the seat for an emergency such as this. Warner took them, but left the half can of tuna—although his by rights—for the Indian. Mrs. Leidy, back in Rubio, had trained him to be suspicious about anything left in a can. Out of the cab he said, "What you might do, when you get into Roswell, is ask the Texaco people to see I get a new fan belt. Some gas, water and a fan belt. Forget his name, man who used to own it, but I've always used Texaco products. Tell him the car is right here west of the bridge, a little less than twelve miles. If he'll toot his horn a bit I'll hear him—I'm just back off the road, on the rise."

Blackbird looked in the direction Warner pointed, seeing what Warner could no longer see. The wind wheel, if still there, might be visible. The cabin would not. Along through here Warner had kept his eyes on the water in the Pecos, like a crack in the earth. There was always something. There was always the dread that it might dry up. Even before he had left, the weather had turned the cabin the color of rusted iron; no color proved harder to see unless it snowed. The two windows in the house were around to the front, facing the west, where the sunsets were like the mountains on fire. A good thing about sheep was the way they soaked up the blazing noonday light. "I'm off about a quarter mile," he went on, "road leaves the highway just beyond the bridge. I don't plan to use it. While I'm here I'll walk in and out."

It was good that Warner knew Indians, or Blackbird's silence would have disturbed him. "I want to thank you for your company," Warner said, but with his hands full, as they happened to be, he didn't offer his hand to Blackbird as he otherwise might have. He noted the hint of stubble along Blackbird's jawbone. That surprised him. Did it mean his blood was mixed? The blast of the diesel horn, although two hundred yards away, led Warner to throw up his arms but seemed to paralyze his legs. Blackbird had to reach out and jerk him off the highway as the westbound van, throttling for the grade ahead, went by with a wind stream that rocked the Maxwell and sucked the breath out of Warner's mouth. The deafening roar of the throttle made it pointless to curse. A cloud of diesel exhaust veiled off the sky, through which they could dimly see the van lights twinkling. "Shhhheeeeeeeee-*it!*" Blackbird hissed, and Warner took off. Walking head down, gripping the carton of Fig Newtons, the canteen swinging on its strap to sweep the ditch grass, he recalled the black man in the gas station back in Nevada who had banged his finger with one of the tire irons. "Shhhh-eeeeeeeeeeee-it!" he had cried. Warner had thought it was air escaping from the tube. It was a new curse, not to be mistaken for the old one Warner tried to spare the ears of the boy. The black man had had it, the red man had it—was it a new way of cursing the white man? He avoided glancing back until he reached the bridge and had the partial concealment of the girders. He did not see Blackbird. The door of the car still swung open on the ditch side. Was he seated in the cab, spearing the smelly tuna with the blade of his knife? Something about George Black-bird appealed to Warner, but something about this appeal disturbed him. The fact was it relieved Warner to realize he had not, in the confusion, said good-bye to Blackbird, nor shaken his hand, implying that they had seen the last of each other. He re-gretted that he hadn't mentioned to Blackbird that fish left in tin cans might be tainted, but he was re-assured to feel that that was something he could smell out for himself, like a dead cat.

SEVEN

This bridge Warner was crossing proved to be a new one, without the planks he could peer through at the glint of the water. They had also made it wider. People who didn't know better might think it was a road. In the past Warner would stop on the bridge for the view it gave him up and down the Pecos. It was almost a canyon: over thousands of years the stream had cut a deep crack into the earth and rock. Viola refused to believe that. This river and canyon, in her opinion, had been made by God, like everything else. Warner had once sent her postcards of Carlsbad Caverns showing stalagmites higher than houses, made by the drip of water over millions and millions of years. He couldn't grasp it. Over him she had always had the advantage that she didn't *need* to grasp it. There it was. The Lord had made it. That was that. What a strange thing it was that his love for her now seemed to be the greater for it. Downstream to the south—it took him time to see it, the canyon being in shadow—the townspeople held picnics where the stream was blocked by old car bodies, dumped off the bridge. They had weathered and rusted to the color of rocks. On those days the kids would climb around on them, and the men would sit there, angling for trout. He recalled that Muriel, although part Indian, never cared for fish because of the bones. She liked the canned sort better, such as sardines, tuna at the time being too expensive. To his knowledge she had never tasted the fish he had bought to feed to the cat. Neither had the cat. George Blackbird, who thought of it as surplus, now had it to himself, if it was what he wanted. Why was it, he wondered, his mind turned to things with which he couldn't cope?

West of the bridge, he dropped down into the ditch grass to make sure he wouldn't miss the turnoff to the ranch. It had never been much: two rutty lanes. More than thirty years of weeds and neglect, allowing for a few vagrants, would have covered it over. He could hardly believe his eyes to come on a path grassless as a schoolyard, almost as wide as a road. The gate he had made in the barbed-wire fence —he had to keep stray sheep off the highway—had disappeared. A few strips of rusty wire indicated where it had hung, but the path was barren as a cattle entrance. What had happened? Would he find poachers on his land? For a moment he thought he should go back for Blackbird, but the Indian would only complicate matters. Had people widened the road to get to the river? It occurred to him that that might explain it. Over the low rise ahead, where the road narrowed, it would dip to a point almost level with the water after the floods. But from the rise he could see that the road continued toward his ranch. Picnickers and fishermen had used it this far, leaving their litter and empty beer cans, but they had built their fires in the river's backwash, a jungle of half-buried timber and driftwood. They had never lacked for wood, but they often lacked for wood that would burn. In search of it they would sometimes follow the path to Warner's ranch. Muriel might give them, or sell them, enough kerosene to start up a fire. Sometimes all they wanted was matches, having come out with no more than what they had in their pockets to light cigarettes. Almost forty years ago

Warner had seen the start of what was now taken for granted. Young people who didn't know what to think, or how to act, not having been told, and lacking examples. After a few years of that they would naturally think they were *free* to think, and do, as they wanted: the problem seemed so elementary he could only marvel why it seemed a problem. He had turned to stand with the prevailing wind, the same wind still prevailing, at his back, the last grain of dust blown from the cracked earth at his feet. Gazing in the direction from which he had come, he seemed to see his life mapped out before him, its beginning and its end, its ups and its downs, its reassuring but somewhat monotonous pattern like that of wallpaper he had lived with, soiled with his habits, but never really looked at. A piece of this paper—he couldn't tell you its color, only that it was darker where their hands touched it, lighter behind calendars and under hooks where clothes hung —Muriel had herself put on one wall of the kitchen to make the room brighter dark mornings and evenings, although the rest of the day she drew the blinds at the windows against the light. He thought it queer, himself, to come in from the yard and see the bright colors on one wall only, the rest of the kitchen, and the walls of the bedroom, the natural dark hue of the wood previously used in bridge construction, and available to him without the cost of transport.

In the direction Warner gazed, a truck with a clattering tailgate, the sun glinting on four or five jangling milk cans, approached the bridge so slowly Warner was sure that it meant to stop. The truck looked so old it might be owned by an Indian, or some local rancher who would let an Indian drive it. It dropped from sight crossing the bridge, and Warner just assumed it had stopped for Blackbird. The clatter of the tailgate continued, however, and the truck reappeared on the slope to the west, the sun flaming on the dirty cab window. It puzzled Warner to see local people not bother to stop. Even if the cab was full, or a woman driving, there was room for the Indian at the back with the milk cans. It testified to how suspicious and unneighborly people had become. Warner felt this was largely the doings of hippies, some of whom were known to be crazy, but whether crazy or not, one thing led to another— one thing led as if willed to another—so that little happenings, on reflection, could not be described as accidental. The wind pressed at the small of his back like a hand, almost enough to lean on, to feel the support of, until the sound of it replaced the clatter of the tailgate in his ears.

The path he followed dipped sharply toward the river, then rose to the rim of the bluff where he had once bailed for water when his well dried up. At that point, as if a machine had collapsed, he found an assortment of iron wheels, one of the largest mounted on an axle across two wooden horses, a gulley trenched in the earth beneath it so the wheel would turn freely. To the outside rim of the wheel cans of various sizes had been bolted or wired. What did the builders have in mind? The river was thirty feet below, even during the season, but near the lip of the rim water from a spring darkened the earth. Weeds had sprouted to help hold the crumbling soil. Were there times—*had* there been times—when it formed a stream to drive a water wheel? No, it seemed more likely that the wheel had been used to catch the water and elevate it. Had the project been completed or abandoned? In the brush to one side he saw twisted lengths of roof gutters. Had they planned to irrigate? He recalled pictures in a *National Geographic* showing how it had been done in the Nile Valley and other biblical lands. It had impressed him as both primitive and resourceful, a notch or two above the local Indians. From the look of it, however, the gutters twisted, this irrigation project had been abandoned, but not before it had worked. A piece of the desert had been cleared and a crop of stunted corn marked the furrows that had soaked up the available water. Not much come of that crop, but it had been planted, so he was faced with the problem of squatters, of *squatters' rights*. Whatever the law might say, Warner himself was sympathetic to those who salvaged what others had abandoned, who took over and used what had been vacated. Migrants, more than likely, Mexicans or Indians, or a family of Okies out of the South or Texas; if they had taken it over, could they have it? He hadn't thought that far ahead. He stood, not thinking, listening to a sound like the rustle of grass, but he knew it to be water. As the water in the Pecos lowered, there was a point where the sound dropped to a rustle as it washed over the stones and gravel in the bed. He walked on to where a blowout had widened the trail at the top of the rise, a fine powdering of sand blowing into his face as he approached. Through half-lidded eyes, his gaze partially averted, he peered over the hump into the hollow where the sheep and their ewes often gathered to get out of the wind. It was now grassless, like a play yard,

119

and strewn with the bodies and parts of wrecked cars. The colors of black and rust, in the morning light, made him think of prehistoric monsters, this hollow a place where they came to die. Beyond, just above his eye level, the slope below the house had been terraced in the manner of rice fields. Where water had settled and evaporated, it gleamed like exposed rock. A few shriveled plants were still supported by sticks; others had collapsed to lie in the dust. The house was there, or more accurately the cabin, to which lean-to shelters had been added, open to the yard. These stalls faced the southwest, were roofed with boards and tin, and sheltered parts of car bodies that served as furniture. The door of a sedan provided one room with an up and down cranked window; he could see that it was down. Torn strips of material that once might have served as awnings stirred in the breeze that always followed the sun's rise. The bands of color looked festive, like banners at roadside stands. Where was everybody? Was it so early they had not got up? He peered around for a dog before moving closer. The wind brought him the tinkle of glass chimes. Light glinted on the strips of glass and tin suspended on wires in the open doorway. A cart made of buggy parts, using the tree and the axles, featured old car wheels with tire casings wired to the rims. Lengths of rope, attached to the front axle, were tied to a yoke that could be pulled by men, rather than horses. Directly fronting the house, where the terraces began, large cylindrical objects, like metal jars, were suspended on wires between heavy posts. The jars were graded in size, and put Warner in mind of the pipes of an organ, or something to be hammered. There was every sign of life but life itself, which he felt must be just out of sight somewhere, as if out of mind. At the top of two long tilted poles, reaching into the sun's rays, several gourds were hung from a crossbar, one of them slowly revolving. As it turned to the sun he saw a small bird enter one of the egg-sized holes.

To alert the dog—if there was one—he hallooed. No response. He moved to where he had a frontal view of the house, where the door stood open, loose on its hinge. The flapping of something attached to the roof was audible. He called again, moving slowly forward, but the silence seemed more threatening than the sound of life. He stood as if waiting to be greeted, glancing furtively at the clutter around him. A piece of a harrow, consisting of four blades, had been left at the end of the plowed furrows. A board

inclined on a log appeared to be a teeter-totter, the
two ends polished by sitting. A galvanized tub and
two chipped enamel pans sat to the left of the door
stoop, one pan powdered with the husks of some
sort of seed. Chickens? The dry strip of the yard had
the look of a pen picked clean by them. He looked
for feathers and saw them in the chicken wire at the
base of the house. Had it been used to keep the
chickens in, or out? The idea of chickens, however,
relaxed him: only reasonably normal people fooled
around with chickens. He called, "Anybody home?"
in a neighborly voice, then walked forward to stand
in the draft of the door. Wind through the boards
at the back filled it with the low moaning sound of a
gourd. That being a sound with which he was familiar, he was not disturbed. Day and night he had
lived with it, but he had never grown accustomed to
it. Familiar but not accustomed. "That goddam
wind," he would mutter aloud, then come to the
door, listening to it. If he feared what he had better
sense than to fear, he would fear the wind.

Thinking of the wallpaper, the one wall that had
it, he peered across the room, empty of objects, to a
scene like fragments of a peeling circus poster, flashes
of garish color, parts of bodies, dangling strips of

what had once been flags or banners, but at the center of the mess, the words printed on a towel, the towel framed by long-tasseled ears of Indian corn:

WHEN THE GRASS IS PULLED UP
THE SOD COMES WITH IT

Warner stood for some time reflecting on the meaning of what he had read. The style of the printing was remarkably flowery—so much so that it gave him trouble to read it—tendrils and flowers worked into the design in the manner of a piece of framed tatting. Mottoes of this sort, usually of a religious nature, had once been tatted by his sisters and sent to him, framed, on Christmas. THE LORD IS OUR SHEPHERD —having in mind his sheep—was one that he had especially detested. His wife had taken them from the frames to insert calendar views of the heads of horses. She loved horses. On a sheep ranch there was not much to do with a horse.

On the floor of the room, set back against the wall, an assortment of car cushions provided beds, places to sit. He could hear mice scurry in the darkness beneath them. Remnants of clothes, shoes without laces, were scattered about as if left by children. The door to the room at the back had been removed and placed on bricks to provide a low table. Pages from a calendar were strewn about as if torn off in a bunch. The smell of the place was dry and clean, like a cob shed, but the old man hesitated to cross the threshold. His own life here had been displaced by a life, or lives, recently departed. He felt their presence. He knew about, but did not strongly feel, his own. The words printed on the banner seemed to speak to this feeling, but somehow remained elusive. Who had pulled up the grass? What was meant by the sod?

He turned away to see the oil drums at the corner of the house, and one rang dully when rapped with his knuckles. There was water at the bottom. When he kicked the barrel it stirred with life. His boyhood fancy that the white hairs from a mare's tail would turn to snakes if put in a barrel of rain water led him to peer, apprehensively, into the barrel's murky bottom. It stank of slime. Slime always stirred with life. Both the garden to the south and the terraces at the front had been covered with topsoil brought up from the river. Had it proved too shallow? Had they had too long a drought? In the cart made of car wheels and buggy parts there were several flats of seedlings that had never been planted. Had it been nature, or *human* nature, that failed them? In what way were they different? The seeds that crumbled in his hands were some sort of beans. Those big metal jars suspended between the posts proved to be brass shell casings. What was their use? The way they hung there invited Warner to pick up a stick and bang on the large one. Hit sharply, it gave off the sound of a gong. Had it been used for pleasure, or some practical purpose? In his ignorance he felt a curious longing. He wanted to know. In his boyhood, and later, farm hands had been called to dinner by the ringing of school bells, the firing of rifles. Like the motto on the wall, these gongs served a less practical purpose. The boy would have liked it—the boy and his two impractical friends. The old man did not believe, he refused to believe, in the hocus-pocus of the dim-witted, but he would have liked to ask the boy what he thought of this apparatus. Ask him. When he gave it a bang see the look on his face.

He squatted in the morning sun, the boards warm at his back, now and then taking sips of the canteen water. By now, surely, Blackbird would be in Roswell. In a matter of hours the tow truck would come for him. He would hear the honking. He would hear the rattle of the tow truck's chains. Curiously, he had given no thought, once the car would run, where he would drive it.

Only one thing is the same as he left it, and he feels

it support him like a hand at his back. If he tilts his head it will moan in his ear like a conch shell. Not so heavy as water, it had proved harder to fight. It seemed wiser to live with it. The wind's invisible will had blown him away, and blown him back. Given time it would work its will on everything it touched, as surely as fire: the works of man disappeared into thin air or went up in smoke. Viola had told him this all her life long, the wind being the invisible will of God, but what she had failed to tell him was that when he came to see this, to know it as the truth, he couldn't care less. God's will and the wind's will were all of one piece.

Back on the plains Viola had gathered around her the ruins and remains of numberless people, some of them believing they would end up in heaven, as she would, or be kept forever in storage, as in a deep-freeze. All of it was now ashes that the first good rain would mix with the earth, and the first strong wind blow away as dust. That he had no earthly use for all that had been lost both pleasantly dazed and amused him. If he had no earthly use, what other use might there be? For Viola there had been no end of the line, since it was on this line she dangled from heaven. In all her long life she had never conceived of a dead end. In all his long life Warner had taken it for granted, but he had never fully grasped its implications. Dead ends were forever. Forever was a thought he could not grasp. The ridiculousness of living forever was not to be equated with being dead forever. No, no. The dead were real in a way the heavenly hosts were not. He could see now that the very presence of the boy had distracted him from Viola's admonitions. He had read these letters to the boy, and through the boy's eyes they were remarkably silly. All of *his* life lay up ahead of him. Nothing lay behind. It was the presence of the boy, tiresome at times, maddening him to a fury at others, that had spared him, until now, the humiliation of the end, of the *dead* end.

He let himself down, out of the wind, on the spring seat of a buckboard. Not his either. Part of a disembodied wagon. His agreeably befuddled state of mind took pleasure in idle fancies. This place was a graveyard. He was one of the many curious objects. Others would be added. The meaning of this escaped him, but he was pleased. From the packet he took one of the Fig Newtons, but found that the cookie coating had crumbled. He didn't really like figs. The boy would eat the cookie crumble by wetting his finger, rolling it in the crumbs, licking it off. Just the thought of that made him thirsty and he took a swallow of the canteen water, the spout shiny with tuna oil and smelling of fish. The smell of the fish brought the Indian closer: why should Warner find that reassuring? It seemed to Warner he could see him licking his fingers, like a raccoon. It was not Warner's nature to be suspicious, or apprehensive, or troubled by darkness like most people, it being what he knew, not what he didn't, that put the fear of God into him. What he knew now should have done that, but it did not. He had given no thought, once the car had stopped, when it might start, or where he might drive it. His thinking had stopped when the car had stopped. It had not started up. One thing led to another. Since morning they had led to where he was, and nowhere else.

Unaware that he had dozed off, he awoke thinking of Pauline Deeter, widow of Arnold Deeter, no children. Lived in the Luau Travel Court in Ojai. Warner himself did the luaus, an expert on the timing of the charcoal fires. The court was near the ocean, and once a week they would gather for a big luau on the beach. Pauline Deeter shared her trailer with an older woman who needed a companion. Warner had felt it a pity a younger woman spent so much of her time with elderly people. She also worked with retarded children in one of the towns neighboring Ojai. On the luau evenings Mrs. Deeter helped Warner set up the tables and keep things going. He liked her kittenish humor. At the sight of her back he knew she had turned from him to smile to herself. In his letters to Viola he had mentioned Mrs. Deeter, her helpful ways. "You old fox!" she had answered. "Are you looking for someone to take care of you in your old age?" The element of truth in that hurt him. He hadn't thought of it in that way, but perhaps he was. They were so often together, and got along so well, newcomers to the court assumed they were married. This rumor disturbed Warner more than it did her. She called him Floyd soon after their first meeting at a square dance evening in Laguna, but he had only recently been so bold as to call her Pauline. At this particular luau, early in September, they were on the beach early to watch the sunset and sing along with Mitch. After the luau it was their custom to sing a few hymns. It astonished Warner how these grown-up people loved to sing hymns. He had detested hymns from the time he could hear the strident, baying voice of his father singing such

129

favorites as "Brighten the Corner" and "Nearer My God to Thee." He had refused to sing them at that time, or later, but he found it was possible to sing them in the company of Pauline Deeter, on the beach. How did it happen that he knew many hymns the others didn't know? He had a good, if untrained, voice. Pauline so reminded him of Viola—getting so emotional her eyes filmed over—he had felt free to assure Viola that she was just like one of the family, excluding himself. As they were waiting for the moonrise, seated on straw mats, out of the blowing fumes of the charcoal, Mrs. Deeter told them all her story about the blind child with the Seeing Eye dog. It was a sad story, about how the child thought the dog was as blind as he was, and when he found the dog had eyes, he hated the dog. The point of the story was, on reflection, that the child wanted to share the dog's *affliction*, more than the dog's good eyes. Mrs. Deeter frequently told the story because there were often newcomers to the luau. That night they had a fine time, as usual, and Warner was gathering up the coals for toasting marshmallows, which they liked to do over a hollow he had scooped in the sand. He was off to one side, with two of the older ladies, when he heard Pauline ask if they would like to hear a touching story. That was unusual, since she had just the moment before told one. They were anxious to hear another one, however, and gathered around her. "There was this poor blind child," she began, "and his Seeing Eye dog." She then went on to repeat the story she had just told them, but Warner did not stay to hear the last of it. One of the ladies beside him, a Mrs. Wohlheim, whispered to her companion, "My God, Lily, there goes Pauline!"

A dead end? Not the death of his wife, which he accepted, but this death in life that he could not, was the first dead end of Warner's life. There goes Pauline! There—but for the luck of it—might have gone Floyd Warner. How many mornings, or evenings, would he have looked up to see her, her eyes still bright, her face unwrinkled, as she patiently told him, for the umpteenth time, the sad story of the blind child and the Seeing Eye dog. What was left of Pauline, with no sign of going, he understood might go on, and on, and on. One day she would have seen, facing her across the table, this strange old man. In a gesture he had always thought very touching, her small, womanly hand would finger the buttons of her blouse. She had a well-formed figure, enhanced by the smallness of her hands and feet.

Fate had spared him, he wrote Viola—which she would interpret as the hand of God—but he did not go on to explain what he had been spared. A man of his age and cranky habits, accustomed to living by himself and resenting intrusions, had no business, he wrote, asking a sweet, gentle woman to share his life. "You wily old thing!" she replied. "I just know it wasn't *your* old age you dreaded sharing—it was hers! Your loving sisters spoiled you. You realize that? I just hope you can make it up to Muriel *later!*" "Later" was Viola's word for heaven, knowing how much he disliked seeing or hearing it mentioned. He knew that she waited to discuss *this* problem, later, with Pauline. "You're such an old *curmudgeon*, you're going to try His mercy—do you realize that?"

Had he come to realize that?

He sat facing mountains he could no longer see, wondering if by now the snow gleamed on them. From this position, gazing westward, he felt at home. Light reflected from the sun-baked yard, but the air was not hot enough to shimmer. He was warm, his body like a potato baked in its skin. In the old days he might stand in the open door, but he seldom sat. He had never been a sitter. Muriel would say, "Now you sit and rest," but he never did. Within the range of his gaze, and his eyes were good, there had always been something that required doing. Was the near-sightedness of old age a cunning way of nature to discourage work, encourage sitting? Out of sight was out of mind. "It would help if you chewed," Muriel once told him, her brothers all being smokers and chewers. How could a woman kiss a man with a chew in his mouth? One thing his father said he had never forgotten, although he had never for a moment believed it. "I was offered a kiss and a chew on the same day of my life, and I chose the kiss." Perhaps he did. No one ever doubted his taste for ladies. In that inherited trait his only son took a certain reluctant pleasure. But he would have liked it better if his taste for ladies had been entirely his own. Muriel had been the first girl he met with an equally responsive taste for men, although her Indian nature was not so responsive as he would have liked. She was willing. His eagerness was something she seldom shared. He felt a drop in her interest when she seemed certain there was nothing much in it for her but pleasure: pleasure being an emotion she accepted, but not one she highly valued. She was willing, he was content, and they shared the durable creature comforts. In the winter one bundle. In the summer apart, on separate cots. He felt rising in him the admission that the warmth of her body was what he remembered, as he now felt the warmth of the sun. Other details—her face and her eyes, the whiteness of her scalp where her black hair parted—like the landscape before him, receded into the receding horizon, a ripple in the thin burning air, up in smoke.

EIGHT

The backfiring of a truck, on the grade behind him, cracked as evenly as an automatic rifle. A drying wind but no sun. He felt its warmth on the lids of his eyes. Out with the herd he had carried a rifle with him, on a sling, but within a few weeks the game knew its range. They looked close enough to him, the critters, but they proved to be at more than one hundred paces. He learned to arch his shots, holding his sight down the barrel to note the wavering flick of the bullet. On one occasion he found the lead pellet, blunted by a rock. One day, in its terror, a big jack rabbit bolted toward the flock where the dog had corraled them, leaped into the air, then hopped from back to back as if the flock were a woolly mattress. No one would believe that. Muriel had not believed it. Even the dog had not believed it. But as he wrote Viola, as sure as God made little apples that rabbit had leaped from back to back of the sheep, like a stone skipping on water. Had *she* believed it? "There isn't a day," she wrote, "God doesn't speak to us through His creatures." That meant she did not. The only person who might have believed it was the boy, but he also might have felt the old man was "losing his marbles," as he had heard him comment about the mailman. Where had he heard it? Who had thought it up? A mind rattling like a gourd, losing its marbles. Fear that the boy might jump to such a conclusion kept Warner silent on such stories. He did not want to see in the boy's eyes the equivalent of "There goes Uncle Floyd!" Was he, in fact, losing his marbles? He could not recall what had happened to that rifle. A Winchester automatic. Finest gun he had owned. Gone with the wind.

Traffic he could hear, but not see, bounced the light around like a mirror. His father had used a pocket mirror to signal to farm hands working in the valley. He had pointed out to Floyd, the one time he had listened, how the curve of the earth could be clearly seen in the clouds. On the plains they receded in a series of steps, conforming to the earth. His father had also noted that the flatness of clouds, at the bottom, was due to the heaviness of air at the earth's surface, and the way they billowed into cumulus masses made it clear that the air was lighter in space. He also believed that up *there*, somewhere, he would live happily ever after. Deliberate father of seven children knowing that his wife would die in childbirth. Would George Blackbird say that he had *killed* her? The word "kill" held no terrors for him. What did hold terror for him? Would it be the word "death"? It pleased Warner to think that the word "death" might disturb *him* less than it did the Indian. Recalling Blackbird, thinking about him, he had the curious impression that he was where he had left him, either in the cab of the car or stretched out in the sparse ditch grass, napping, this being the time of day it was foolish to do anything else. Warner needn't trouble to formulate it, but what they had in common, now, was waiting. The day having started, now they waited for it to end. Beyond that, Warner could not push his thought any more than he could push the stalled Maxwell. A dead end.

The tips of his fingers placed on his eyelids resulted in a series of overlapping halos. He could not determine on which side of his eyelids they seemed to be. He reflected on the mystery of seeing on the mind's eye. From exactly where he sat he had fired his rifle at a timber wolf made reckless by hunger. A shift in the wind had blown the smell of sheep and roasting meat into the wolf's face. Warner could sense his torment: how much more he knew than he was able to see! Hunger had brought him so close to the fire Warner could see the graying beard on his long muzzle. An *old* wolf. He understood better what might have made him reckless. Not necessarily hunger. Not necessarily anything he understood.

In the dusk, painfully, after being seated so long, he got to his feet and looked for firewood. This took him to the rise with its view of the highway. The white girders of the bridge appeared ghostly. If there had been the smoke of a fire he would have seen it. He stood there wondering if that reassured him. In the dry bed of the river the rusted body of a car tilted on boulders to provide a shelter. Would Blackbird be there, crouched on his hams in the manner of an Indian? For what was he waiting? Was he waiting for Warner's dead end? It gave him more satisfaction to admit that than it had given him to conceal it. It figured. It had not come to pass by an accident. Somewhere in the shadows, or under the bridge, Blackbird crouched watching Warner, and waiting. Strange that the thought of it aroused in Warner emotions, impulses that were reckless, like those of the wolf. He was tempted to tilt back his head and howl, but he did not: not for an Indian. Blackbird would smile. To himself he would say, "Foolish old man, what do you want?"

What *did* he want? He wanted no more than what he had found.

It pleased him to slowly gather materials for a fire. There were pieces of twisted driftwood in the yard that he knew to be there for some ornamental purpose. Around on the backside of the cabin (why the *back?*) steer horns and skulls found out on the range had been stored on the roof. For what purpose? He had no clue to their purpose. Something Indian in his wife (nothing else seemed to explain it) led her to gather up smooth or colorful rocks and place them, like plants, on the sills of the windows. He sensed in this childish habit some deep inscrutable meaning. The sun shone on them. They soaked up what otherwise might be lost.

In a widening arc, to the north and west, the scrub

had been cleaned of anything that would burn. He recalled that some of these long-dried shrubs burned with the colors of Christmas baubles, and gave off a strong scent. As the slopes around him darkened, the sky brightened, providing a softly luminous, indirect lighting. On the highway the westbound cars had turned on their lights. To the east, arching over Texas, the feathery tracings of jets still burned in the sun's rays, but he did not see them, nor the low bank of smog that had drifted or blown here from somewhere, like the exhaust of a grounded rocket. It startled him to see the moon, the lower half illuminated by the setting sun, looking no farther away from him than the horizon. This moon did not seem to arise in space, but to emerge from a slot in the earth behind the mountains, thin as a coin. The haze gave it the glow of a pumpkin, like the harvest moons of his boyhood. He once saw as well by the light of this moon as he did by the sun, perhaps better. There was less glare: he was able to see moving objects quickly, and judge distance. In this light a flock of sheep were like one body, feeding on everything at its circumference. The sound of the cropping, on a windless night, was like that of boots treading crisp snow. The flock itself sometimes moved like a sleeper stirring in sleep. At such moments the stupidity of these creatures seemed less oppressive to Warner, each one being but a small part of the larger, vegetative monster, let out to graze at night. He imagined there might be such vast creatures on the floor of the sea.

In the shelter of one of the tilted car bodies he carefully assembled scrap for a fire. It had been Warner's custom, acquired back when he lived here, to carry kitchen matches in the buttoned-down pocket of his shirt. These matches cast a light bright enough to see by, and a half-burned match, with its charred tip, served as a flame-cured toothpick with a charcoal taste. He now recalled—finding his shirt pocket empty—that he had given his last match to the hippie, and with that match the lamp had been lit that set fire to the house. "You got a match, Pop?" the kid had asked him, and Warner had freely given him his last match. Now he turned from the fire he could not light to think of the one that match had started. Without that fire he would be back in Chapman, curled up asleep in a bunk of the trailer, the boy a lump like a sleeping dog in the bunk overhead. Without that fire all that had happened to Warner would not have happened. The prayer circle of old women (and the spell they cast on him), the grave of Ivy Holtorfer, a white boy killed by Indians, the kitten in the outhouse, George Blackbird in the restaurant, the long day of waiting, and the fire he had built but had no match to light. The meaning of that both intrigued and escaped him. He reflected on it with a puzzling satisfaction. One match had proved enough to leave the present in darkness, illuminate the past. One thing had led to another, and all of it led to where he crouched in the yard, as if he had planned it. Wasn't that what he had wanted? That things should go according to some plan? That however they went, they should not be like ditch weeds fitfully blown in the wind stream of a car. He had been agitated by Blackbird's manner, but he had welcomed the sense of foreboding. He had been free (so it seemed) to choose the white bum, and they would now be as far as Albuquerque, or Gallup, but in point of fact he had not been free to choose one or the other—he had been chosen. Was that so strange? Not so strange as it first seemed. If he went back over his life, as he had been doing, as it seemed to have been planned that he had come here to do, he saw that the crucial decisions, the meaningful choices, had invariably been made by others; his choice had been in conceding that their choice had been right. Viola's will, not his own, had led him to take the boy, and the boy's will, not his own, had led him to pick up the hippies. In these reluctant decisions his own will had been challenged, and lost. In losing he had hoped to hold on to something he valued more highly than his will. The love of Viola; the affection and respect of the boy. George Blackbird, however, challenged his will in a matter that seemed outside of these considerations—outside, in a way that appealed to him, of himself.

Was it true that the black eyes of red men saw better at night? Blackbird approached the house slowly, as if looking for something he had lost. In his right hand he held an object that sometimes glowed like the lens of a lantern. Did he think to see by it? Or to signal? Tilted upward, it reflected the moonlight. He seemed so absorbed in his meandering, Warner appeared to play no part in his calculations. Perhaps it just pleased him to wander by moonlight. At that point where his shadow lengthened he called out, "Old man, where are you?" His tone was familiar. One might have thought that the term "old man" was one of affection.

"I am here," Warner replied. Did Blackbird see

him? The moon shone impartially on the clutter. Blackbird lifted his head in the manner of a man accustomed to smelling better than seeing. When he moved, however, he came along a line that pointed directly at Warner. With each swing of his arms the object in his right hand flashed the light, like a predictable signal. On the baked slope of the yard he cast a shadow so pale it seemed to lie between him and the ground he walked on. The spirit of a man made visible by moonlight. Ten or twelve steps away he stopped abruptly and said, "You no build a fire?"

"I built it," Warner replied, "then found I had no matches. Left my matches in the car." In Blackbird's silence he sensed the judgment that here, too, white and red men differed, the red man not needing a match to start a fire. He said nothing, however, but crossed in front of Warner to the unhinged door of the house. From the pocket of his coat he took Warner's flashlight, directed its beam into the room's corners. He saw it flash dully on the glass at one window, flare briefly at the cracks in the walls.

"Like a war," Blackbird said, "they leave nothing."

"They left it better than they found it," Warner replied. "They did a lot of work. They tried to irrigate it."

"You think war is no work, old man?"

He stepped into the room, kicking at some of the car seats, then crossed it to peer into the room at the back. He was there for some time, returning to the door with what appeared to be part of a fishnet. The dangling strings of the net were tied to strips of tin and glass. "To fish?" he asked.

Warner did not think so. "A piece of fly net," he said. "We used to have a horse."

"Could be yours, could be theirs, could be mine," said Blackbird.

"You can have it if you want it," said Warner. "Help yourself." It amused him to think what Blackbird would consider an object of value. He held the fly net before him, so the glass and tin dangled, rocking the net in such a manner the glass tinkled. "You hang it where the wind blows. It makes a wind chime."

"Not for this you come back," said Blackbird. "Right?"

This word, like the clothes on his back, was something he had picked up in the Army. It had its use. It was one of the few things he had not left behind. There was a rudeness in the word, a challenge, that Warner clearly sensed, but it did not arouse him.

Aloud he said, "Right!" "Right!" the Indian replied.
Into Warner's mind popped Viola's comment that
it was *his* nature to expect the worst. What was the
worst? How did one know it when it occurred?
"Now we've had the worst," Viola often said, meaning that whatever it was, they had survived it. So it
was something that went from bad to worse, but did
not go on forever. The despair that had seized him in
Viola's bedroom at the farm had no bottom to it, no
name, no handle, but its presence had been so over-
whelming it had stopped his breathing, like a weight
on his chest. How true it was to speak of being in the
grip of death! If there was order in this world, or in
Viola's heaven, it was at such a moment Warner
should have died, having experienced the worst. It
was at such a moment the devil got in his licks, but
here he was, a day later, worse off but feeling better.
The faintness of this feeling, almost pleasantly giddy,
was in part due to the fact that he had not eaten, and
the long day in the sun. "The sun's got to you!"
Viola would cry, if he said something unusually
foolish. He often did to encourage her to say it. What
lively times they had had together. Aloud he said,
"What's that you got there?" and pointed at the
object in Blackbird's right hand.

Blackbird gave it a buff on his coat sleeve, then peered at its surface as if for his own reflection. What he saw led him to sniff it. "Fishy!" he said.

What childish delight, Warner wondered, did the Indian get from the lid of a fish can? A pocket mirror? The ragged edges of the lid were razor sharp.

"Mr. Blackbird," Warner asked gravely, "you mind my asking what you plan to do with it?" The Indian seemed to ponder the question, testing the edge with the tip of one finger.

"Razor sharp," he said.

Warner was touched and amused to note this aspect of Blackbird's nature. The lid of a can served him as a mirror, served him as a knife.

"Old man," he said, calmly, "give me your hand."

"I know it's sharp," replied Warner. "Sharp as hell. You think I don't know that?"

Blackbird's hand remained extended toward Warner, the palm up, as if expecting an offering. In contrast to his squat, short-legged figure, his hands were small, the fingers long and slender. A boy's hand, Warner would have judged it, more than a man's. Was this why—against his will, or if not against his will, against his better judgment, against something instinctive in his nature—he put forward his own hand,

147

the palm up, as if Blackbird meant to read it by moonlight. The Indian gripped it gently, his fingers at the back, his thumb firmly pressed into the heel of the palm, and with a gesture so deft Warner scarcely saw it, flashed the lid of the can so that it caught the moonlight. Warner felt nothing but the increased pressure of the thumb in his palm. The blood that flowed into his palm, black in this light, he thought must be from the hand of Blackbird, one of his strange and disturbing Indian customs. He looked up to see why he had cut himself.

"For christ-a-mighty's sake," he said, pulling both hands toward him, where he saw that the blood flowed from his own wrist. It pumped, as if a leak had occurred at his pulse. The Indian continued to grip the hand, firmly, the thumb pressing to the palm as if to slow the bleeding, the dark blood filling, then overflowing the cupped palm. Did Warner cry out? Not to his knowledge. Pain might have aroused or disturbed him, but he felt no pain. The hand that gripped him, the thumb's steady pressure, seemed to bring to one spot all of the life in his body, there for him to observe.

"Mr. Blackbird—" he said, but hardly in protest. Out of wonderment, perhaps, out of clarification.

"Old man," Blackbird replied, "you sit quiet and you live longer."

That amused Warner. Did Blackbird feel that was his concern? As if taking his pulse, his thoughts elsewhere, Blackbird had turned to face the rising moon, stirring Warner to marvel at what might be on his Indian mind. Had he been a good soldier? His cunningly laid plans were well carried out. From Warner's watch pocket he would take the timepiece that had stopped sometime during the morning, a gold-cased watch with a movement so weary it would run something less than twenty-two hours a day. Warner had learned to give the stem a twist each time he looked at the time. In the pocket of his shirt, the flap buttoned, he would find eighty dollars in ten-dollar bills, and maybe ten to twelve dollars in his wallet. Otherwise, nothing much of value. Several clippings sent to him by Viola about the death of people in and out of the family, at least one of which had encouraged him—without mentioning names—to outlive the bastards. In many ways he had. About George Blackbird, who would survive him, his feelings were more complicated. Step by step, as if Warner had helped him plan it, all the pieces fitting neatly as a jigsaw puzzle, the Indian had picked up his scent and tracked him down to where he was lying, his wound self-inflicted, the razor-edged can lid lying in his lap. Faintly, due to his weakness, Warner felt a twinge of admiration. A passer-by, if there had been one, would have said that the red man had paused to help him, and stood holding his hand. On Warner's mind's eye he saw this scene—one of the last he would see—as if clearly painted. It would bear the somewhat puzzling title "Old man, what do you want?" From the scene it seemed clear it was help that he wanted, but he seemed reluctant to ask for it. What help? All his life he had made it a point never to ask. Everything had happened according to a plan that would prove to be his as much as Blackbird's, so that what he wanted, strange as it might appear, was what he had got. That would prove to be even truer of Blackbird, who now took from Warner such things as he valued: the money from his wallet, the watch from the bib pocket, a knife with a blade less sharp than a can lid, and from the canteen, dangling on its strap, enough of the water to rinse the blood from his fingers.

These movements of the Indian affected Warner like the ritual of the prayer circle. A presence known to him, outside of himself, noting his weakness and